PANIC IN THE AIR

There was a hint of madness in Creighton Thornesby's calm-sounding voice as he discussed his plans. The Penetrator moved in closer to be sure he missed nothing. . . .

"I'm going to launch Phase Two immediately," the doctor declared. "Phase Two involves a viral agent that will cause a rare form of influenza to spread all over the country. Once the first few cases are spotted, the farther apart the better, it won't take long to convince everyone there is a dangerous national epidemic. Given a week of that and the public will be ripe for our nonexistent 'right-wing extremist' group's ultimatum."

Two major questions remained unanswered. How, from Wisconsin, did Thornesby intend to spread a flu epidemic across the country? And what sort of ultimatum was going to be made?

Hardin had better find out fast . . . before the crazy scientist began his final countdown to terror. . . .

THE PENETRATOR SERIES:

#1 THE TARGET IS H
#2 BLOOD ON THE STRIP
#3 CAPITOL HELL
#4 HIJACKING MANHATTAN
#5 MARDI GRAS MASSACRE
#6 TOKYO PURPLE
#7 BAJA BANDIDOS
#8 THE NORTHWEST CONTRACT
#9 DODGE CITY BOMBERS
#10 THE HELLBOMB FLIGHT
#11 TERROR IN TAOS
#12 BLOODY BOSTON
#13 DIXIE DEATH SQUAD
#14 MANKILL SPORT
#15 THE QUEBEC CONNECTION
#16 DEEPSEA SHOOTOUT
#17 DEMENTED EMPIRE
#18 COUNTDOWN TO TERROR
#19 PANAMA POWER PLAY
#20 THE RADIATION HIT
#21 THE SUPERGUN MISSION
#22 HIGH DISASTER
#23 DIVINE DEATH
#24 CRYOGENIC NIGHTMARE

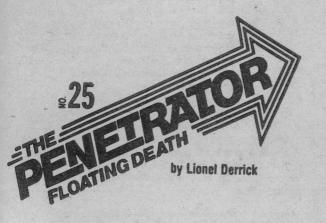

THE PENETRATOR

No. 25

FLOATING DEATH

by Lionel Derrick

PINNACLE BOOKS   LOS ANGELES

Permission to quote from Bert Ward's article, "The Bombing of North America!" granted by the publisher, *American History Illustrated*, Gettysburg, Pa.

PENETRATOR #25: FLOATING DEATH

An original Pinnacle Books edition, published for the first time anywhere.

Special acknowledgment to Mark Roberts

ISBN: 0-523-40178-7

First printing, April 1978

Cover illustration by George Wilson

Printed in the United States of America

PINNACLE BOOKS, INC.
One Century Plaza
2029 Century Park East
Los Angeles, California 90067

To Laurie Rice, the best-looking pilot I've ever met; and to Don Cox . . . for old time's sake . . . don't break any more legs.

CONTENTS

	Prologue	1
Chapter 1	Official Slaughter	9
Chapter 2	Packer's Punch	23
Chapter 3	Sinister Printout	37
Chapter 4	Unhealthy Interview	43
Chapter 5	Other Battles	57
Chapter 6	New Allies	65
Chapter 7	Casualties	73
Chapter 8	Captive	87
Chapter 9	Abrupt Departure	95
Chapter 10	Midnight Move	103
Chapter 11	Saturation Technique	109
Chapter 12	Traveling Doom	117
Chapter 13	Modified Answer	127
Chapter 14	Crack Up	137
Chapter 15	Plague Farm	147
Chapter 16	Black Death	159
	Epilogue	171

FLOATING DEATH

PROLOGUE

*Pale death approaches with an equal step,
and knocks indiscriminately at the door . . . .*
                                            —Horace

As it is decreed, all good things come to an end.
So it was for Mark Hardin. The once nearly
frozen Joanna Tabler lay warm and cuddly at
his side, and the tropical sun still burnished their
bronzed bodies; yet Mark knew it was over—
ended as surely as the bulky package delivered to
their room that morning. It was a wrap-up on
Preacher Mann and his icy escort business.
Worse, confirmation that the cunning, evil black
man was far from content with escape. The
Penetrator felt sure he would hear more from
Preacher Mann. In the meantime, there were
other things of importance demanding his attention. Mark opened a copy of *U.S. News and
World Report*, turning to the article he had read
that morning.

At first glance, the article had struck his interest. It wasn't so much what it was about—a crisis
in the dairy industry in Wisconsin. Farmers were
always experiencing crises. What interested him

1

was the cause of the tempest. Several deaths had occurred from contaminated milk and dairy products in Madison, Oshkosh, and Milwaukee. It sounded to Mark like a repetition of the PPB scandal that had devastated Michigan. Mark had called the Stronghold and asked Professor Haskins to accumulate everything he could on the strange, widespread disease.

Mark Hardin was the Penetrator. Only a rare few living people knew this, for his secret had to be well maintained. It was all that allowed him to travel freely to any part of the nation or throughout the world. The press had first put the name *Penetrator* into play back when Mark was slashing and hacking his way through the ranks of Don Pietro Scarelli's Mafia family in Los Angeles. It had been a personal thing then. Unwittingly, Mark and Donna Morgan, Professor Haskins's lovely niece, had brushed close to something the Mafia bigshot preferred to keep unknown. As a result, Donna died in the flaming wreck of Mark's car on a lonely road up near Big Bear Lake. Mark mourned Donna, but the world went on. By the time Mark finished, had Donna Morgan been a Valkyrie, she would have enjoyed an incredibly large retinue accompanying her to Valhalla. In the aftermath, Mark, Professor Haskins, and David Red Eagle—an unbelievably old, unquestionably wise Cheyenne medicine man who had taken charge of Mark's physical rehabilitation following his beating in Saigon—formed a crime-fighting triumvirate, dedicated to smashing the skulls rather than slapping the wrists of the bloated parasites who enriched themselves—most often with impunity from high in the political sphere—by sucking the vitality from the little guy.

Mark was no stranger to ugliness, to death and violence. An eighteen-month tour in Vietnam, in which he was assigned to a combat intelligence unit that ran problems through the always-liquid front lines deep into enemy territory, had seen to that. Then had come Counter-Intelligence Corps school in Maryland and another tour in Nam, this time to wade armpit deep in the slime of double agents, corrupt politicians, and the black market. The beating, which had left him broken in body and spirit, was administered in an empty Saigon warehouse at the hands of some of the rotten apples in the army's otherwise fresh and wholesome barrel.

Discharged from Letterman General Hospital in Frisco, Mark was in need of far more than a pat on the back and his country's thanks. His former football coach at UCLA had recommended Willard Haskins and his isolated Stronghold residence in the Calico desert of California. Mark went, reluctant and doubting, to find quiet, peace, and the chance to sleep each night without a cocked and locked .45 under his pillow. His recovery had been painfully slow at first but then livened up with the coming of David Red Eagle, taking on even more meaning with the advent of the dark-haired, gray-eyed vision, Donna Morgan. But Scarelli had unthinkingly ended that and paid frightfully for it.

The Penetrator wanted all those who casually snuffed out life to pay their dues. He killed when he had to, not without careful consideration and conviction, yet totally lacking in guilt or regret. He was what he was and, as he had put it to Terry Lucas in Denver, he happened to be the best there was at what he did. Following the L.A. heroin ring bust, there had been the Fräulein in Las Vegas, with her unsavory nest of vipers. It was a fitting simile, the Penetrator thought, considering what had happened to her.

Then he was on the move across the country. In Washington, D.C., he annihilated the *Société Internationale d'Elite*, an elitist One-Worlder cabal with visions of themselves, naturally, on top and the rest of us grubbing around below serving them. The Penetrator then moved on to New York to bring a fistful of white lightning down on a black militant group that held Gotham hostage in the world's biggest hijacking. But he was picking up scars, both physical and mental. The realization that it couldn't last, that he would make the wrong turn into the wrong alley at the right time and meet his maker in a blast of burning powder and zinging lead, traveled with him as he took his juggernaut to New Orleans. But a Cuban plot to flood the country with counterfeit money and wreck the nation's economy was canned up along with the shrimp soup in Marcel Bouchet's floating factory.

4

After that, the names, faces, and places began to blur, one dissolving into the other: Tokyo; Baja California; Seattle; Dodge City; the Utah desert; Taos and a fight for his Indian brothers; Boston in aid of an old friend; Atlanta; British Columbia; Quebec, with its lead to France; the Bahamas, a nice place for a vacation, but not with pirates at work; a bizarre chain of evil running from Florida to Nebraska to Guatemala, then back to N.Y.; to Costa Rica and Panama for some more of Castro's dirty tricks; a trip to the Rockies to combat a sick gang of world-savers who thought the best way to do it was by killing as many as they could; then to Texas on the trail of wetback slayers; a mad fling with the Oregon Terror; and back to Denver to look into the kinky doings of Vanua Levu and his Church of the Final Coming. With hardly a chance to catch his breath, the Penetrator found himself battling Preacher Mann and the icy certainty of death that the greed-driven black man had concocted for his lovely merchandise.

True, he had enjoyed a longer period of respite following his Florida fandango, the weeks lengthening into one month, two, more. Joanna had come and gone as her assignments required, while the Penetrator basked in the sun and dreamed of a better life—one in which the word pronounced "slaying" was spelled with *eigh* and performed over the crisp, cold fields of December behind a gently clopping nag, to the joyful shouts of happy children.

Despite all the blood and mayhem in his life, such scenes kept returning to Mark's mind, vying with the realization that it was spring and time for the baseball preseason games, his thoughts turning to how his California Angels would do this year. But those images were replaced by other, more somber ones.

Now he concentrated on the mysterious goings-on in Wisconsin. The vine-covered cottage with kiddies running about and the lazy days of sun on an empty beach would have to be put aside. Even the eternal quiet of the grave would have to wait until the Penetrator had thoroughly scratched the curiosity bump that warned him the Wisconsin milk contamination was only the tip of a far worse problem, lying just below the surface. He focused on the page, a frown of concentration deepening as he read.

A U.S. Public Health Service official, Dr. Creighton Thornesby, was quoted as saying that if the offending organism was not definitely identified, its source isolated quickly and eliminated, it would be necessary to quarantine and destroy all herds and close down the entire Wisconsin dairy industry, with resultant severe economic crisis in the state. The alternative was totally unacceptable: contamination of entire segments of the national population.

From the farmers' point of view, the crisis had already come. Several dairymen had seen their herds condemned and slaughtered on nothing more than suspicion. Their protests to Dr.

Thornesby had been to no avail, and because of a USPHS budget deficit, they had not been compensated for the loss of their cows. A delegation had appealed to the state legislature, and yet another group was on its way to Washington. Economic ruin threatened thousands of people. The cheese industry was in a panic.

"You're getting wrapped up in something again," Joanna said, her tone flat, resigned.

"Jo? I didn't know you were awake, honey. I'm not sure what this is," the Penetrator told the lithe, lovely platinum blonde beside him. "It's just . . . something . . ."

"Important. I know."

"First off, I need on-the-spot information. Remember my mentioning Olie Swensen—the guy with the Packers?"

"Oh, sure. You two played football together at UCLA."

"That's the one. Jo, I'm sorry. Really I am. But this thing looks interesting, and I need someone to fill me in. Olaf has a dairy-farming background—in Wisconsin, too. I think it's about time I accept his standing invitation, visit the Green Bay Packers. Harmless enough, isn't it?"

Joanna Tabler made no reply, only looking at her man with longing . . . mixed with a little fear.

Chapter 1

OFFICIAL SLAUGHTER

Cra-a-a-ack!

The shot rebounded tinnily off several metal grain storage bins. A woman whimpered in resignation. Beside her stood a man in faded bib overalls, work-thickened, roughened hands writhing in helpless fury, his weathered face suffused with red, frustrated anger.

A milk cow stood a moment as if stunned by a hammer blow, then blood gushed from its nostrils and mouth, its front legs buckled, and it fell gracelessly to the ground. Other animals in the herd milled about, bawling nervously at the smell of death.

"But . . . chu haf no right . . . " the man protested again in broken sentences, his voice thick with a German accent. "Ve haf the papers, *ja*. Chust last veek comes the inspector. My herd is clean, he says. Now you . . . you *Schweinerei* come und kill off my cows. Ve . . . ve lose everythink. *Alles ist los* . . . the barns, der loan . . . ve lose even the land."

Two other men had joined the white-smocked rifleman. Their next blasts came almost as one shot. Three more black-and-white spotted Holstein dairy cows fell to earth. A fourth man turned in response to the farmer's anguished pleas.

"Your herd is contaminated, Mr. Kruger. Every herd in the Rhinelander district has been contaminated."

"*Aber, Herr Doktor* Thornesby, you . . . you haf said it takes seven to eleven days to incubate, this germ thing."

"There is no appealing my decision. Your herd was reported to us, I investigated, and have decided they are infected with whatever it is that is tainting the milk. People have *died*, Mr. Kruger. Doesn't that mean anything to you?"

"*Und* my cows are dying, Dr. Thornesby. Healthy cows who do no harm. *Und* with them my life. Only for a suspicion? How can this be? *Verdampten Schweinhunde!* From since my family brings me here as a boy to be free of that *verückter* Hitler, we live in peace, haf work and plenty. Now . . . now you come *und* suddenly Hitler's ways are in the United States. Where is justice, I ask you?"

The guns crashed again, and three more of Karl Kruger's cows died—golden, tawny Guernseys this time, from his special "cream" herd. They had been docile, placid, affectionate beasts

10

in perfect health. Kruger groaned with anguish, and his wife sobbed openly. Their youngest child, a boy of thirteen, stood beside his mother, confusion masking his face as silent tears streamed down his cheeks.

"Make it faster, men," Dr. Thornesby commanded, turning indifferently away from the stricken family. "There's three-hundred cows here and two more places to get to. The bulldozer will be here later to dig a hole for these animals," he went on, addressing his remarks to Kruger. "You should be glad you will not have to pay for the burial."

Mechanical proficiency, like the butchery of the Kulacks by the Red Army, finished the job in less than an hour. The U.S. Public Health official and his men climbed into their vehicles and raised a thin stream of dust behind them as they hurried on to their next appointment with a doomed dairy herd. Kruger was shaking with suppressed rage, his face deeply lined. His wife had retreated to the house, and his son had run to the barn to hide his grief.

"*Bei der lieben Gott*," Kruger swore to the heavens, "this *Herr Doktor* goes too far. Ve do not live in a police state. You shall be stopped, Dr. Thornesby—if I must do it myself!" Heavy booted feet stirring dust in the farmyard, Kruger strode resolutely toward his battered pickup. A roiling plume of dust formed a horizontal exclamation point behind his truck as Kruger set in pursuit of Dr. Creighton Thornesby.

11

It was late afternoon before Dr. Thornesby and his grizzly assistants finished their day's slaughter and returned to the Regional Public Health headquarters in Wausau. Night fell and ten o'clock came before Thornesby arrived at an old farm outside Medford, Wisconsin. No lights shone in the windows of the aged, shabby farmhouse. Thornesby pulled through the yard and stopped beside a crumbling barn. The once-red paint had peeled long ago, leaving only smatterings of the carmine coating on gray, weathered boards. Thornesby waited five seconds, then lightly tooted his horn twice.

A bullet-headed, keg-shouldered man, carrying a shotgun, came from a small door at one side of the barn front. He peered into the darkness, then approached Thornesby's car. As his eyes adjusted to the difference in light, he recognized the visitor.

"Oh, it's you, Doc. C'mon in. Mister Wen is here."

"Very good, Randy. It's nice to see you are so vigilant."

Inside the musty barn, which smelled of moldy hay, Creighton Thornesby's pale features split open in the whitely gleaming grimace he considered a warm smile. "Ah, Theophilus, old friend."

"Good to see you, Creighton. Your men here have just finished a complete tour. Most impressive, even if I don't fully understand it."

Theophilus Wen's short arm swept the interior

12

of the crumbling old structure, taking in the thick blankets of insulation and sound-dampening material covered by tar paper that sealed off all but the slightest random light or noise leak. His stocky body and faintly Oriental features moved with excited agitation as he indicated the gas-generating plant and stacks of cartons, all government surplus, identified by bold black letters as containing "BALLOONS, METEOROLOGICAL, MARK IV." At a white table, protective masks in place, surgical gloves and smocks guarding them, men filled one of these gray-purple weather balloons, adding a substance from a smaller cylinder, which had never been intended for inclusion by the makers of the synthetic-skinned gas bags.

"You should be wearing protective clothing, Theo."

"Don't fear, I'll not be going close to where they're working. Tell me, any accidents so far?"

"None. I have a most competent crew here."

From over near the preparation area, nerve-jangling rock music was interrupted by the smooth tones of an announcer, and the workmen paused to listen to the radio report.

"Winds of ten to fifteen miles per hour from the northwest are pushing our slight promise of rain beyond this region, giving hope to Iowa and southern Illinois tonight. These winds will increase to twenty-five miles per hour, with gusts up to forty, continuing into tomorrow. No rain in the forecast, with tomorrow's high sixty-four,

13

the low tonight, forty-two. Stay tuned to WKEB for the latest news from around the world every hour on the hour and our local weather picture each half hour."

"Perfect," Creighton Thornesby said, rubbing his hands in anticipation. "That weather report," he explained to his visitor. "Gives us a chance to determine patterning. By this time tomorrow there should be sick cattle from here to Urbana, Illinois." In the background the National Weather Service advisory station played continuously on another set, giving a running report of conditions across the nation.

"What about the seven or more days incubation?"

"Smoke screen, Theo. It's merely to keep the public guessing. That's a highly virulent bacterial agent we're using. Actually, twenty-four to forty-eight hours is more like it. When an outbreak begins, it gives us up to twenty-one days to move in on healthy herds in adjacent areas, using the seven- to fourteen-day incubation story as a cover, once we've determined the financial condition of the farmers involved. Your conglomerate has been able to purchase the places it wanted without difficulty, hasn't it?"

"Easily. All we had to do was offer a little more than anyone else was willing to lay down."

Creighton Thornesby rubbed long, slender fingers together in a sign of pleasure. His pale features took on an inner glow of satisfaction, and his gaunt, pigeon-breasted frame seemed agitated

14

with approval. Here was revenge and profit in the same stroke. It tasted sweet indeed. His words, when he spoke, seemed addressed to some inner self, rather than intended for other ears. Low-wattage, yellowish light from a battery of electric lights refracted in sharp-edged splinters from his thick-lensed eyeglasses.

"They said it couldn't be done. Shouldn't be done. Conquer a nation by the economic control of its production, distribution, and retail sales of food. That's the project they set up, gave to me. Then they said stop, no more. Bacterial agents should not be used in a world already so troubled by starvation, they sanctimoniously cried. I'll show them, those green-suited hypocrites at Dougway. If they feel it's immoral to use it on an enemy, we'll see what they think when I use that method on this country." He stopped, sobered, looked at Theo Wen. "But I'm rambling again. My discontent with the tunnel vision of the army and their so-called scientists at the Utah proving ground are of no interest to you."

Nor to any of us, Wen thought. Bringing a powerful nation to its knees simply to make them see the error of their thinking over some inconsequential germ warfare project was far too simplistic for the survivors of the *Société Internationale d'Elite.* Seven of us . . . just seven. Wo doesn't count. The fool and his Triad Society: the *Chiu Chou.* Secret hand signals and rule by the hatchet—Oriental daydreaming. It had taken years, though, for the few who had avoided direct connection with SIE to rebuild their power base, located this time on solid, sound business principles.

They literally floated their way to their present status on a lake of Arab oil—transported on *their* tankers, sold through *their* brokerages, refined and distributed throughout Europe and the States by *their* companies. It also provided one important step toward eventual domination of the country . . . and through it the world. Their strong finger on the pulse of the petroleum industry could, when the time came, also be used to stop that flow, bringing industry and transportation to their knees. Now those billions would be used to gain control of the production of all foodstuffs in the nation.

Creighton Thornesby had proven an excellent tool to use. His concept of dispersing bacteriological agents by surplus weather balloons came at precisely the right moment and as nothing short of inspired. Giving Thornesby a modestly impressive portfolio of stock in the conglomerate through which they were operating insured the man's loyalty. They needed that fidelity to achieve their goal.

Less than thirty percent of the nation's population was engaged in agriculture. Reducing that figure to nearly zero would give the remaining SIE members what they wanted. Private ownership of the land, of America's farms, was a stumbling block to SIE's plans. Once crop and livestock losses forced most of the farmers out, nothing would prevent them from completing the chain: from the raw product to the retail outlets. Food prices would soar, bringing the people to the brink of starvation. Then the final blow—the threat of using the silently drifting death against large population centers and the seat of government itself. That would deliver absolute political power into their hands. The thought pleased Theophilus Wen. He smiled warmly as he clasped Thornesby's arm.

"What interests me," Wen said, picking up the threads of their conversation, "is this system of yours. How does it work? How safe is it for us?"

"As safe as can be. Don't worry yourself. Everything is contained within the proper cylinders or in the balloons. Nothing . . . untoward . . . can happen."

"I was thinking of once the balloons were released."

"Not a chance. But come on, I'll explain it to you," Thornesby urged, drawing his guest toward where the masked men were inflating a balloon. "You see, there are two separate inlets, one from a cylinder containing helium—which we have made here on a surplus military field generating unit—and the other from a far smaller container of the concentrate bacterium. I call it a concentrate, but actually it is highly diluted and becomes more so when released into the air. In order to adversely affect a human being, at least in sufficient enough concentration to prevent use of an antitoxin, you would have to ingest the entire contents of one of the small phials of the culture starter that are kept in that locked cabinet on the far wall. Even then, a counterserum I have developed could be administered with the effect that the victim would have nothing more than a runny nose and severe headache.

"Now, to get back to my point, each of the ingredients is under pressure and flows freely through regulators into the balloon." He turned away to the workmen. "Watch how many psi you put in those balloons. They have a long way to travel, and that means constantly increasing altitude. We don't want them bursting before they reach Illinois."

"Isn't there a danger of explosion here?"

"Hardly. Helium is inert. The balloons can't burst accidentally. They were designed for the military for use over-enemy as well as friendly territory. So one design feature was a self-destruct system. The simplest is to have the air bag rupture from a difference in pressure. We fill these to a predetermined capacity, so that they will rise and explode from internal stress at the altitude we want them to. I've already explained to you how safe people are from the airborne contaminant."

"Good enough . . . if you're used to this sort of thing," Wen admitted, edging away from the work area. "By the way, your list of prospective front men for purchasing farms in the southeast part of the state has been screened and approved.

There will be a large amount of cash coming in within the next two or three days for their use, some $475,000. You will have to be responsible for it until it is disbursed to them and the farms are in escrow."

"Nearly a half million. I suppose it is as safe a place here as any to keep all that cash. . . ." Thornesby's comments were interrupted by a startled shout and a brief struggle from outside. As he and Wen turned toward the source, the barn door opened. The guard, Randy, stood behind the form of a man in bib overalls, menacing his captive with a sawed-off shotgun. He prodded the prisoner forward into the light.

"Ah! Karl Kruger, I believe," Thornesby said evenly, working hard to cover his consternation at the seeming ease by which their security had been breached.

"So—so, it is you behind this *ungeheuer* thing!" the angered farmer blurted out when he recognized the man who had supervised the slaughter of his cattle that morning. "*Und* for *money*—you take money to destroy us . . . our farms, all we have lived and worked for. With my bare hands I would kill you."

"Not likely under the present circumstances, *Herr* Kruger. Step on over; I want to show you precisely how we do it."

"I have heard it all. I know what you do here, why. You are monsters, madmen. I will tell it all to the law, the police will come, and then we see who is doing what."

19

All the while Kruger spoke his denunciation of Creighton Thornesby, Randy shoved the farmer from behind with the butt of his shotgun, forcing Kruger forward. Thornesby, meanwhile, selected a small phial from a rack of similar glass containers in the locked cabinet he had pointed out earlier. He shook it until a milky substance in the bottom blended with the other contents. Then he picked up a hypodermic needle, checked its sharpness and condition, and filled the syringe, turning to Kruger.

"You must have spent the entire day following me, Kruger. Not very wise. No, indeed. Almost as stupid as blurting out how much you knew of our little operation. As it is, you can't really think I could be as foolish as you. Turn you loose to talk, all that? Oh, no, my bucolic friend. You are going to be the first direct victim of this new livestock plague. Providing proof, at the same time, that I acted wisely in killing off your herd this morning. Your death will be a beneficial turning point in my campaign. Hold him," Thornesby commanded the guard.

Strong hands grasped Kruger, his shirt sleeve was pulled up, and Thornesby's needle stung its way into flesh. The farmer struggled, but to no avail. A virulent concentrate of the bacteria being spread by their deadly balloons, the effect of the toxin was rapid and startling.

Within twenty minutes Kruger's eyes began to redden, water; mucus ran from his nose and lips. He shivered and winced as a massive headache manifested itself. Licking dry lips, he tried to speak. "Wha . . . what haf you . . . done . . . to me?"

"We have killed you, you meddling fool. In approximately two hours you shall be dead. Your death will be attributed to the bovine toxin, the proof of that cause being that you are a dairy farmer. Oh, yes. In a very short time you will be a corpse, I shall be very rich, and Mr. Wen here shall rule this country and through it the whole hemisphere."

Chapter 2

PACKER'S PUNCH

"-- . / . - . / - ... / *Green Bay VOR* ... - -. / . - . / - ... / *Green Bay VOR* ..."

The high-pitched, measured shriek of Morse code alternated with the emotionless, unaccented monotone of a disembodied human voice, identifying the Green Bay, Wisconsin, VORTAC navigational aid over the cabin speaker. In bright white letters, the figures 117.0 showed on the "To" Nav receiver of the King KFC200 Silver Crown flight control system as Mark Hardin depressed the "Com 1" toggle; the radio it was connected to displayed 119.4 for Green Bay Approach Control. He punched the "Transmit" button on the yoke and spoke into the slim boom mike poised an inch in front of his mouth, identifying Mooney N201PB.

Approach Control handed Mark over to the tower, on 118.7. Mark punched the frequency in and keyed his mike. He identified himself and was told to squawk 1220 on his transponder. After resetting the altimeter and programming his approach and back course into the KC292 Mode Controller, the ATC in the tower at Austin Straubel Air Field now "legally" flew the airplane.

After touching down on runway 24L and taxiing to the ramp at Executive Air flying service, the Penetrator arranged for hangar space for his new Mooney 201. It was, he felt, a transitional airplane. The Mooney wouldn't handle the payload his Duke had hauled around with ease, but it definitely could fill the bill for most missions the Penetrator set out upon. With Preacher Mann on the loose and the description of Mark's multi-engine Beech known to him and who-knew-how-many other criminal organizations, it would have been madness to keep the Duke. The big bird sat where he had landed it, in the hangar at West Palm Beach, Florida, a for-sale sign in the window and instructions for the operator of the flying service to sell it and send the money to one of several blind-drop postal addresses Mark maintained. It was a safe enough procedure, for the incoming items were sent on to a mail-forwarding service that in turn dispatched them to yet another dead drop. Built-in warning systems allowed the Penetrator to fold up the entire operation if it were compromised at any point in the chain. Confident of a quick sale on the

Duke at a bargain price of $375,000, Mark went in search of a new means of swift transportation.

Like all airplanes, the Mooney 201 was a compromise between load capacity and efficiency. The 200 hp Lycoming and super-streamlined design allowed a cruise speed of 195 mph with fuel consumption of 18.1 mpg. It was economically sound, and the big engine used gasoline so sparingly and efficiently that it made ecological sense as well. That got the Penetrator around at a respectable speed, for an astonishing range. The real problem lay in cargo capacity.

Flying alone, as the Penetrator usually did, allowed for an additional 590 pounds useful load. That took care of his covert tools: the lightweight aluminum luggage in matched sets that carried an assortment of weaponry from a diminutive High Standard .22 Magnum derringer to an awesome M79 grenade launcher. Each pair of the four suitcases contained a complete arsenal. But special equipment was frequently needed, and it required hidden storage space. To accommodate it required some modifications.

Mark had the rear seat removed and a boxed-in compartment installed, covered with carpet matching the interior decor. On top of this construction, as added cover, he had installed a bolted-down typewriter and a slant-deck reel-to-reel tape recorder. Both were battery powered—a World Traveler model Smith-Corona and a Sony recorder. Behind its hidden entrance, with access only through the rear lug-

25

gage compartment, Mark stored enough explosives, ammunition, and larger weapons to start a small war. It took a big man to handle all these munitions, and the Penetrator filled the bill.

Mark Hardin was a large, powerful man. His six-foot, two-inch, large-boned frame was heavily muscled, yet managed to retain the lean, hungry look of an athlete bound for the Olympics. His normally dark complexion was suntanned a coppery brown from his extended R and R in the Florida Keys, his bright, intelligent black eyes and white teeth flashing in the broad, high-cheekboned countenance. He could move with the litheness of a cougar, and his heavy brows and prominent hawk-billed nose gave his face, even in repose, a smouldering, critical look. When he frowned, his full lips turning downward, a cold aura of death seemed to hover over him.

Mark's hair was black, grown a little shaggy after his isolation from civilization and barbers, once more hiding part of his ears and brushing occasionally against his collar. His usual weight of 205 pounds was maintained without conscious effort or diet. When he spoke, his words were well modulated and precise, delivered in a neutral, network newscaster accent, but Easterners and those from the Deep South soon picked up a slight far-West twang if they listened closely. If those auditors were enemies, however, they never had a chance to listen that long before they were dead.

Though many had died in blazing confrontations with the Penetrator, none of this showed on Mark's face as he locked the Mooney, taking along three metal suitcases from the luggage compartment, and left the flight service hangar.

Over the Unicom channel to Executive Air flying service, he had ordered up a rental car from Avis, and it was waiting for him when he came out of the office. A sketch map of Green Bay, done in red mimeograph ink, accompanied his rental papers, with the location of the nearest motel marked, as he had requested. Starting the Cutlass, he nosed out of the parking lot and headed toward Airport Drive.

Two miles beyond the point where Airport Drive turned into a freeway, Mark swung onto the offramp for Ashland Avenue. Crossing back under the freeway overpass, he made a right into the parking lot of the Southwest Holiday Inn. He checked in, took the key for room 144, and headed there to set up shop.

Mark's room was ideally situated, on the ground floor of the back unit, overlooking the inner courtyard and swimming pool and beyond it the restaurant, lounge, and back entrance to the office. His parking place was located so that it could not be seen from the street. Altogether a neat, anonymous home away from the Stronghold for the Penetrator. He entered, unpacked, laid out a yellow legal pad, and began to plan his campaign.

27

He located the address of the Green Bay Packers offices—1265 Lombardi Avenue—and phoned. After two false starts, Mark's call was handed over to Shirley Leonard in the PR department. Yes, Olaf Swensen should still be in the building. Who was calling?

"This is a friend of his from California. I used to play ball with Olie at UCLA. He's been trying to get me up here for years. Now that I've made it, I don't have any way of getting hold of him except through your office."

The voice at the other end became a little less distant, warmer. "I see. If I may have your name, please, I'll see what can be done."

"This is Gilbert Latham."

"Was this concerning employment with the team, Mr. Latham?"

"No," Mark laughed depreciatingly. "Not after this long out of the saddle. I had a few days and thought I'd visit with Olie and his family."

"You know his family?"

"Only through letters. Judy and the boys are high priority on Olie's list, I know that."

This was information the typical gate-crashing fan wouldn't have access to. "I'll back that. What say I leave a note for Olie with the receptionist and another with Earl DuChateau? One or the other will reach him."

"Ah, no. Don't mention my name. I want this to be a surprise. Just say he should wait for a few

28

minutes. I can be there in ten to fifteen minutes. I'm staying not far from your offices."

"Fine. I'll do it that way, Mr. Latham."

"Thanks."

Mark replaced the phone and headed for a quick refresher shower. He changed into casual clothes and left his room, turning the Cutlass onto Ashland Avenue, east to Lombardi, and left to the twelve-hundred block. The lot in front of the yellow- and green-trimmed two-story office building was nearly empty when Mark parked. Inside, behind the aluminum and glass cage situated in front of the outer glass double doors, the receptionist took his name and buzzed him through the electric-locked glass panels to where a gray-haired, slightly balding man stood. His body told clearly of former athletic prowess and boded well for current strength and excellent health.

"I'm Earl DuChateau," the former ball player introduced himself. "Things are rather informal around here—just call me Earl. Olie's cleaning out his locker right now. If you'll come with me, I'll take you to him, Gilbert."

"Thanks, Earl. Lead on."

Past the first locked door, Earl waved a hand casually toward an open portal, beyond which Mark caught glimpses of a profusion of stream-lined, solidly built Nautilus weight machines. "That's our weight training room," Earl informed the Penetrator offhand. Over the door was a hand-lettered sign:

29

There is *No* Substitute
for Strength and *No* Excuse
for the Lack of It.

"That's one of Bart's mottoes," Earl explained with pride. "He's got them all over the place." After a pause, "We go in here."

Standing barefoot on the green, low-napped indoor-outdoor carpeting, at the far end of the yellow-walled locker room, a huge-shouldered, bull-necked blond turned from his chores as they entered. Earl excused himself and departed. A Grand Canyon-sized grin split the lantern-jawed Swede's broad face as he recognized his visitor. "Mark! You old son-of-a-bitch, how are ya?"

Mark's features wriggled themselves into an expression of warmth and pleasure. "You never change, Olie—fat, dumb, and happy."

Olie Swensen lowered his massive head, shoulders rolling and bulging with muscle, and charged, checking his mock rush when Mark set himself for the block. " 'Py gollies,' as my Oslo-born grandfather would say, a guy never loses the old touch, eh?"

"Good to see you, Olie. Damned if you don't look in better shape now than the last time I saw you."

"That's Bart's doing. He puts us through a half-hour mandatory workout in the Training Room every day after field drill."

"You gotta hit the iron if you want to be number one."

Olie's grimace was rueful but proud. "Don't I know it. So what brings you to Green Bay?"

They were walking back to Olie's locker now, the second one from the large scale standing beside the doorway to the equipment rooms. Olie reached into a mound of battered practice shoes, stuffing them into a large canvas bag—gold and green in color, of course.

"Business," Mark said. "I'm into paper products out in L.A. and had to stop in on Fort Howard Paper Company."

"You? In paper products? You're shitting me."

"Not that kind of paper, Olie," Mark replied with a straight face. "Besides, your pun stinks."

"Olie grimaced. "God, I thought the army'd cure you of that outhouse humor. Puns is awful."

"Okay, enough, enough. Really, I am in the paper business and I had to come through here, so I thought I'd take you up on your invitation."

"This is the last day, you know. End of season. I'm packing to head north to my happy home. At least it was happy until this damned plague hit."

"What plague is that?"

"This dairy thing. Contaminates milk, they say. The folks are retired, living in town. I'm running the dairy farm on the Flambeau River. At least I will be if that prick Thornesby doesn't decide to slaughter *my* herd too."

"Who's this Thornesby, and what's the story on killing off cattle?"

"Well, now I have a sympathetic ear, I might as

31

well cry the blues a bit. Creighton Thornesby," Olie said, a low rumble in his voice betraying his suppressed anger, "is the Regional Director of the U.S. Public Health Service office in Wausau. He's also a goddamned butchering swine. So far he's slaughtered thirty herds in this state, and only five of them proven in advance to have whatever this fancy new bug is that is contaminating milk and dairy products. I'd like to hammer his skull in a little."

"Hey! Take it easy. Go slow and let me get this straight."

Olie took a deep breath, grimaced, and shook his head to clear his thoughts. "Hell, Mark. I guess I'm just too wound up over this thing. City people believe milk comes in waxed-paper cartons, or plastic gallon jugs. You have no idea how serious dairy farming is to people in Wisconsin. A third of the state's industry is connected in some way to milk and milk products. Cheese, ice cream, dry milk—for God's sake, a million products, even some plastics, start with milk. We'd be hurtin' good if this Public Health edict succeeded in killing off all our cows. But that's not your problem. You gonna come up to the farm?"

"I don't know where it is—and I don't think I'll have time."

Olie looked disappointed. "Heck, it's not so hard to find. We're on the South Fork of the Flambeau River, about ten miles north of Fifield, near the Lac du Flambeau Indian Reservation.

You really oughta come up. Judy'd love to meet you."

"She don't even know me. But how's the fishing?"

"Great! Walleye, Northerns, trout, Coho—you name it. Say you'll come."

"I—well, if I'm not tied up too long on this special order deal, okay. I'll try to make it after I'm through."

"I figure you're as good as there already. I've got a boat, a big beer cooler, and all the fishing gear we need. Don't let me down, now." Olie's mood changed slightly, pride filling him. "How about a tour of this joint? Get a behind-the-scenes look at the Packers."

"I'll take you up on that, no sweat."

"Lemme finish with these shoes. Damn, why a guy wants ten pair of practice shoes, I'll never know. At least you feel that way at the end of the season. All that money spent and half of them not usable the next year. 'Course, I'm not as bad as some of these lunks. Take Mike there," Olie said, hooking a thumb at a towel-shrouded, muscle-bulging black man who stepped from the sauna and padded into the dressing room.

"Mark, this is Mike Butler, number-one draft choice for this last season. These rookies all think they need two dozen pair of practice shoes."

"He's jivin' ya, man. Don't listen to Olie. I only have a dozen pair, not *two*."

Mark took the ham-sized black hand in his own huge paw, giving and receiving a hefty, deliberate shake. "Glad to meet you, Mike. Surprised you didn't make NFL Rookie of the Year."

Mike Butler grinned sheepishly. "So am I. But, then, it's like Bart says. It took him a time of obscurity before he led the team to five straight NFL titles. I got time."

"And you're full up with that," Mark replied, indicating another of Bart Starr's mottoes.

" 'What Kind of Attitude Have You Shown Today?' " Mike quoted. "Yeah, man. Ol' Bart, he's got it all together, no lie."

"I was about to get the VIP tour, Mike. Glad to have met you. And good luck next season."

"Pleasure meetin' any friend of Olie's, Mark. See ya around some time."

Half an hour later, the Penetrator left Lambeau field after a football fan's dream tour of the Packer plant. From the playing field, to the top of the 56,300-capacity Lambeau Field stadium with its aluminum bleacher type seats, to the Norwegian cedar-lined sauna, the Training Room with stacks of York barbell iron and gleaming Nautilus weight machines, the triple-whirlpool-equipped Therapy Room, then upstairs to the conference room. Plays for the Packers' last game were still diagrammed on six soft-green "blackboards." Movie projectors waited silently to be called into service to convey information to the men of the four divisions: offensive and defensive line and both backfields. To one side a modern, well-equipped kitchen provided interruption-free access to nourishment to team members absorbing wisdom from chalk and celluloid.

Back down in the locker room area, Olie ushered Mark into the *sanctum sanctorum*: the coaches' lounge and locker room. Most of the staff was long gone, except for Dick Corick, one of the directors of personnel, who was zipping up a B-4 bag. Another stood before his locker, third in a short row containing Bill Currey's and Bob Lord's cages. Even without the green and gold hand-lettered name card, Mark easily recognized sandy-blond, massive, and grinning head coach and general manager of the Packers, Bart Starr.

Introductions were made, Mark expressed his admiration and appreciation, and Olie secured from Bart a season's home game pass for Mark. A few more words were exchanged, and they made their departure. Mark parted from Olie, assuring him he would do his best to make it up to the farm.

But reunions and sightseeing were over. There remained Dr. Creighton Thornesby and the whole contamination scam. Although Olie had mentioned the Public Health man, and his name appeared in all the articles Mark had located and read, he felt sure this was a person he wanted to learn a lot more about. Something wasn't right about this whole thing. Before another day passed, the Penetrator intended to find out what it was.

Chapter 3

SINISTER PRINTOUT

Paralleling the Fox River on his drive back to the Holiday Inn on Ashland, the Penetrator puzzled over the version of the contamination problem given him by Olie Swensen.

Dr. Creighton Thornesby, Regional Director of the U.S. Public Health Service seemed, according to Olie, to be acting in an autocratic manner. His swift, unannounced descent on dairy herds in the state was inconsistent with the usual meticulous, well-deliberated investigations and follow-up of the Public Health Service and USDA. There was an almost frantic haste in the doctor's actions. This precipitate action gave Mark an uneasy feeling. He'd have to check it out with the professor.

Back in his motel room, Mark placed a call to the Stronghold. Once the connection was made, the Penetrator attached his portable scrambler unit to the handset of the phone and asked for all data available on Dr. Creighton Thornesby. There was a brief pause, then the computer printout began to clatter. Professor Haskins read off the sheet as the machine produced it.

"Thornesby, Creighton Leonard, born February 9, 1926, at Hoville, Illinois. He was the second of five children. Normal home life, attended private prep schools, entered the army in 1944, served with Army Medical Corps, '44–'46. After discharge, returned to Illinois."

"Let's get to the meat of it."

"It's coming, my boy. Patience is still a virtue, even if saying it is a cliché. Ah, here's what you'll want. Thornesby attended University of Illinois in premed, also University Medical School. After he was graduated, he did not take an internship, but remained at the university on a research grant, working in the fields of parasitology and bacteriology. He entered civilian service for the U.S. Army in 1956 at the CBR facility at Provo, Utah. Transferred to Dougway, Utah, Army Proving Grounds in 1963."

"Interesting. But you're behind the times, Professor. When the army made the move to Dougway, they changed the designation from Chemical-Biological-Radiological Warfare to ABC, for Atomic-Bacterial-Chemical. For what it's worth, though, it opens some interesting avenues."

"Oh-oh. Here's something you might find useful. Remember back a ways when there was a big furor over the revelation that the army tested some nonlethal bacteriological agents in six cities in this country? Well, at the time Thornesby received quite a bit of newspaper space when he quit his job in protest. Whether it was over the disclosure or the actual tests, we're not sure. But he did disclaim any knowledge of the events and claimed to be shocked and angry that the army would stoop to such an unethical practice. There were several deaths attributed to the tests, if you recall. A lot of wrangling went on in the House and Senate—demands for a full investigation, a congressional committee, that sort of thing. Then it sort of died down from lack of momentum. After the smoke cleared, Dr. Thornesby went to work for the U.S. Public Health Service. He's been with them ever since."

Mark pondered it a moment. "So, he didn't like the idea of testing germs on our own people. Who did? What does that say?"

"There's more, but it's from my unofficial and unconfirmed file."

"Read on."

"This first part has been verified since it was entered. Thornesby is independently wealthy, owns large amounts of stock in several multinational conglomerates. In particular he has a handsome block, some fifteen percent, of one holding corporation with a large chain of retail grocery stores, packing plants, and produce wholesalers.

"My most recent data, from reliable but unconfirmed sources, indicates that Thornesby was, in fact, the man who suggested American cities for tests of germ warfare devices and had been at odds with the army for refusal to allow research in an area of his own choosing. It seems that what he was interested in was a radical, unorthodox, and dangerous approach to defeating an enemy nation. He went so far as to develop a pilot project before the army said no. No other details as of now, but I'll be on it. As a result of this undisclosed project, though, the consensus among academics who knew him is that Thornesby quit before the army could fire him.

"If I may be permitted to read something into this—purely subjective, of course—which I think important you take into consideration, I would predict this: you will find the man not all too stable. Taking into consideration this supposed project of his that the army vetoed, his indignant resignation over the U.S. germ tests smacks of monumental hypocrisy."

"But it would possibly fit with his conduct here. According to Olie, Thornesby is personally leading a team that slaughters dairy cows out of hand. No quarantine of suspected animals, no testing, simply go in and kill them on Thornesby's word."

"That doesn't sound at all like the Public Health Service. They usually move much slower than that, make sure before committing themselves."

"What's worse, as Olie tells it, there have been no provisions to reimburse the farmers for their livestock. The government is covering the disposal of carcasses, but the dairymen are left to guess about if or when they might recover their loss."

"Most irregular indeed. Perhaps—"

"I'm way ahead of you, Professor. I intend to have a long, searching talk with Dr. Thornesby tomorrow in Wausau. There's one other thing. If Thornesby is acting independently of authority, it could be a paranoid reaction to his experience with the army. Or it could be he suspects a real human agency connected to the wide dispersal of this disease. If the latter is the case, and I'm beginning to suspect it is, then some means has to be used to spread it. Look into possible ways for me, and I'll get back to you tomorrow afternoon. It might tie in with something else Olie told me."

They made brief farewells, set a next contact time, and the Penetrator hung up the phone, replacing his scrambler unit in one of the arms cases. A solid rumble from his stomach reminded Mark that the dinner hour had come and slipped slightly past. The tone of the hunger growls said seafood. Mark checked the telephone directory, located a Red Lobster Inn not far from his motel, on Lombardi Access Road. He armed himself lightly with two High Standard .22 Magnum derringers and left, carefully locking his door.

Mark made the drive to the Red Lobster Inn in ten minutes. As he pulled into the parking lot, he noticed a vehicle blocking the space filled by a

Datsun station wagon. Between the cars a slightly built, balding, bespectacled man was struggling with two thick-shouldered youths. In the front seat of the Datsun, a white-faced woman looked on in horror, her hands pressed to her face. Two small girls, the eldest not over twelve, sat in the rear, screaming out their fear. A quick glance around showed Mark that there was no one else nearby to heed their cries for help.

The Penetrator reacted instantly, braking to a stop and leaping from his Cutlass without thought. As he neared the struggle, one of the pair of thugs raised a meaty fist, fingers wrapped around a short length of pipe. The Penetrator's left arm lashed out, strong hand and wrist arresting the sap-wielder's motion in an iron grasp.

"Now you don't want to do that, pal," the Penetrator said, exerting more pressure, causing the punk to release his grip on the pipe. The mugger's reaction was not as expected.

"Harry, get this turkey offa me!" he cried.

As the words were spoken, the Penetrator heard the distinctive *snick* of a switch blade opening behind him. Before he could release his grip and whirl to meet the new threat, the blade thrust forward toward his exposed kidney!

Chapter 4

UNHEALTHY INTERVIEW

The Penetrator dropped low, knowing it was more difficult to successfully insert a knife blade between the ribs of a moving target than it was to place a paralyzing blow into the soft meat of lower back and kidney. As he did, he swung his right arm backward, pivoting the forearm so that his clinched right fist struck his assailant on the back of his elbow.

The knife blade snagged in the tough fabric of Mark's resistweave sports jacket as Harry gave a yelp of pain and surprise when the bones of his arm snapped. The Penetrator continued his turn to the left, lashing out with his left hand and arm, fingers open and together to drive into the nerve center of Harry's groin, just above the penis, shock paralyzing the young thug into a useless lump of agonized flesh, flopping on the asphalt of the parking lot.

Now the Penetrator gave attention to the

other pair. The nearest one had bent to recover his pipe club but jerked erect as his partner shouted a warning. He turned in time to meet unpleasantness personified. A thoroughly angry Penetrator bore down on him with the swiftness of the Angel of Death.

"Gimme some help, Paul!" he had time to shout before his frizzy orange pseudo-Afro was bobbed around like a freed balloon as the Penetrator snapped a left, a right, and another left to his head. Then he was grabbed by crotch and shirt collar, the Penetrator smashing his head once . . . twice . . . three times into the bumper of the trio's car. Mark dropped his unconscious form like a bag of wet laundry. Then he turned on Paul.

"Come on, Paulie, baby, I got just the thing for you," the Penetrator urged in a low growl.

"Hey, man—what you did to Crock and Harry —that's police brutality. We're gonna get your ass for this."

"Too bad I'm not a cop," the Penetrator said softly as he continued to advance on Paul.

Paul's eyes went wide with fear, and he backed away, arms before him, pleading. The Penetrator closed with him and let Paul get a good look at the dimunitive derringer he had hidden entirely inside his hand. Then the hard voice rasped out, commanding, compelling obedience from the shattered mugger.

"On your knees, punk. Get down! Now, crawl over here and apologize to this man. And to the lady and those girls. Tell them how sorry you are to have disturbed them." Paul hesitated, the Penetrator gestured roughly with the hand holding his derringer. "Do it!"

Paul complied, whimpering with fear all the while. He mouthed a disjointed apology and licked dry lips, starting to say something more, when the lights went out.

The Penetrator delivered a ponderous hammer-like blow to the back of Paul's head, jarring him out of the conscious world and sending the punk sprawling face first to the macadam. Skin abraded loose, and a handful of red seeping wounds appeared on pimply skin. Aware that Wisconsin state law forbade the carrying of concealed weapons by anyone except police officers or the military, the Penetrator quickly and deftly hid his derringer before turning to the man.

"Call the police, mister. And I'd file a complaint if I were you."

"Don't worry about that. You bet I will. We have very little crime in Green Bay. When outsider punks like this come around, it doesn't take long before they get the word. Say, I'd like to thank you, though. I appreciate what you did for us."

"Forget it. I needed the exercise to stimulate my appetite. I'd appreciate it if you didn't mention my part in this. Just get the cops and forget I was here. Good night."

"Uh—yeah. Good night."

Mark walked away, toward the door of the

Red Lobster Inn, visions of oysters on the half-shell and King crab legs dancing happily in his head.

When Mark left the restaurant, fully sated on seafood, he was puffing contentedly on a *Presidente Palma*—Mexico's finest cigar—completely at peace with the world. He paused in the shadow of the building, thrown by large lot lights, and gazed upward. Despite the size of Green Bay, it was surprising how many stars could be seen. Nothing like the desert around the Stronghold, the Penetrator thought, but a respectable display for all the lights. He started toward his car, only to stop, his mind recording a movement seen by his eye a fraction of a second before. He looked up again.

Shielding out most of the parking lot brightness with cupped hands, he focused on the dark object that drifted through the night sky. Yes, that was it, a weather balloon. It had to be. Carefully he searched the area around it. There was another, a third. But why no reflective material on the instrument packages so they could be tracked by theotolite? And why three of them? Well, it was no secret about the extravagance of many government agencies. Mark dismissed the incident from his mind and headed to his Cutlass.

As he neared the rental car, Mark noticed a black and white Green Bay PD unit off to his right, sitting on the lot. It waited, no doubt, for a wrecker to haul away the Chicago car that Harry,

Crock, and Paul had used. The officer nodded to Mark in a friendly manner, light glinting off the silver badge on his light blue short-sleeved shirt. Then he removed his white eight-sided garrison cap, wiping at the band.

"Sure warm for this time of year," the broad-shouldered cop said.

"You know it. Looks like an early spring," Mark replied as he slid behind the wheel of the Cutlass and eased from his parking space. After the little foray with the muggers, the last thing the Penetrator wanted was an extended dialogue with the long arm of the law.

Early the next morning, Mark rented a Granada at Wausau Municipal Airport, where he'd flown in the Mooney, and drove into downtown Wausau on Grand Avenue. He had purchased copies of the *Green Bay Chronicle* and Wausau *Daily Herald*. Both newspapers headlined stories on the discovery of the body of Karl Kruger, a dairy farmer from the Rhinelander area, some miles north of Wausau. Dr. Creighton Thornesby was attributed with stating that it was apparent the dairyman had died of the same mysterious contamination that had infected Wisconsin dairy herds. Kruger's body was found in his pickup truck at the side of a country road not far from his farm.

Thornesby also was quoted as stating that the unfortunate farmer's herd had been disposed of the previous day due to the presence of the disease. Mark tuned in a news broadcast on WRIG, listened to an abbreviated version of the story. To the Penetrator, this event made his visit to Creighton Thornesby even more important.

Mark easily located the federal office complex in the Marathon County courthouse. That impressive edifice occupied an entire block, bounded by Forest, Sixth Street, Jackson, and Grand. Mark was momentarily amused as he walked past the door to the FBI office, wondering what Howard Goodman and his Penetrator Squad would think if they knew that the man they sought so unsuccessfully was less than twenty feet from one of the Bureau's lairs. U.S. Public Health Service occupied a corner portion of the second floor. Mark gave the receptionist his current cover name, Gilbert Latham, a freelance writer, and followed directions into Thornesby's office.

"Ah, yes, Mr. Latham. A writer. In view of what's going on up in this country, I have little doubt what you want to talk about."

"Then we have a meeting of minds already, Dr. Thornesby," the Penetrator said. He smiled disarmingly. "But when I tell you I'm doing an article for *Dairy Herd Management* out of Minneapolis, that might not be the case."

"No worry on that account. I understand and sympathize with the dilemma this places dairymen in."

"Just what is this disease?"

48

Thornesby shrugged, spreading his palms depreciatingly. "I honestly can't say."

"But haven't you obtained samples, something the labs can work with?"

"Yes. But so far, no results. Some sort of mutated bacterium, they say. What ever it started out as, this strain has so radically altered that it is so far unidentifiable." He laughed, sharing an inside joke. "Some of the more science fiction-oriented technicians have even suggested germ warfare."

Thornesby had given the Penetrator the opening he had hoped for. "You were formerly connected with the Dougway Project, weren't you, Dr. Thornesby?"

Creighton Thornesby froze a split second, eyes narrowed. His voice carried all the warmth of a January northeast Wisconsin wind. "The errors of my youth, I'm afraid. Yes, I did work in the ABC project at Dougway. My public denunciation of their unconscionable acts and subsequent resignation seem to have done little good, however. I shall no doubt be hounded by that reputation to the end of my days. But surely that's not to be the main thrust of your story."

"No, sir. Just a little background—your expert ability to handle such situations because of your former employment, that sort of thing. Try to cool down the hotter heads among the dairymen. There's fear the plague will move out of Wisconsin."

"No chance of that, young man. We have it tightly contained."

"Ah, that's the kind of thing I want. This farmer," the Penetrator went on, abruptly shifting conversational gears, "Kruger? The one found dead in his truck. What can you tell me about him?"

Again Thornesby tensed, his demeanor growing more distant. "No comment. Beyond what I've already released to the press, it's too early to tell anything."

"Is he the first known case to die from direct exposure?"

"No comm—well, I suppose it can't hurt anything. Yes. He is the first one so far as we know. But we can't rule out the possibility that he obtained it the same way the other fatalities did. The family no doubt consumed raw milk from his cows. His herd was destroyed yesterday, you know."

Mark nodded. "Have you checked out that possibility?"

"I had intended going up there today, but—" Thornesby waved at a stack of papers littering his utilitarian GSA-issue desk—"things stack up. I'll dispatch a deputy to inquire into it."

"I see."

The Penetrator asked several more general questions for form, then left the office. There was something definitely hinkey about Thornesby. He had been evasive and acted oddly, particularly when Kruger was mentioned. For a public servant, doing his job as he believed best, the doctor had no need to feel pressure in this area. It gave the Penetrator more to ponder.

After checking into a motel, the Exel Inn, Mark phoned the Stronghold. Professor Haskins had nothing more on Thornesby. There was a late-breaking story concerning an outbreak of the same disease among dairy herds and beef cattle in northwestern Iowa and southern Illinois. The news was a blow. Thornesby had assured the Penetrator that the plague was contained. He'd have to put aside the problem of the nervous doctor for a while. Concentrate on the source.

"Okay, Professor. Not that I like the sound of that. Now, what can you give me on some means by which this disease can spread so rapidly? Did you dig up anything yet?"

"Not much, my boy. Really hardly enough to make a report."

"Considering how much territory it has skipped between outbreaks, anything might be important."

"Very well. There is one way, but one would have to be dealing with an enemy of the country to make it valid." Willard Haskins sighed, hesitantly. "An article appeared in the December 1976 issue of *American History Illustrated*. It was written by Bert Webber and was about the Japanese balloon bomb campaign in World War II. Far-fetched in this circumstance, but if you can locate a copy, read it. It might give you some ideas."

"Balloons?" Suddenly random incidents clicked into place in Mark's mind. "Wait a minute. That's what Olie was telling me about. His Indian workmen on the dairy had commented to him about an unusual number of weather balloons being located, burst, on the Lac du Flambeau reservation. And last night I saw a flight of three. They didn't look normal to me. Then today, Thornesby said some of his lab staff had jokingly suggested germ warfare. But that's ridiculous. Who would be doing it and why? How could it be carried off?"

"Seems from this article that balloons were released from Japan and used the jet stream to drift across the Pacific Coast. Some went off, others were duds and recovered. It was a highly classified secret for a number of years. I'm sorry there's nothing much else I can do now."

"Well, it's a place to start, Professor. It might tie in with our hypothesis that Thornesby suspected enemy action." The Penetrator sounded unconvinced. *Balloons.* Even if they were being used, how could they escape detection? But it was a lead, and it tied in with Thornesby's unusual reaction. He made his good-byes and started back to the center of Wausau. Perhaps the library would have a line on such a use of balloons or other devices.

Mark located a copy of *American History Illustrated* in the Wausau library. Bert Webber's article, "The Bombing of North America!"

proved far more interesting than he had expected. The Japanese balloon project, code-named FUGO, or "Windship weapon," was devised from an earlier one dusted off in 1942 after the Dolittle raid on Tokyo. One paragraph in particular, on page 36, caught the Penetrator's attention.

.

One of the first threats U.S. investigators believed the balloons posed was the carrying of biological agents—germ warfare—to America to spread disease. Hastily formed balloon (and bomb) recovery teams included intelligence officers, demolition men, and chemical warfare experts. Dressed in massive "space suits," the team probed everything with poles and clamps. When all Japanese materials were tested, including snow samples packed in dry ice from mountainside recovery sites, no evidence of biological warfare agents were ever found. Interviews with General Kusaba in 1963 and with Tanaka in 1974 and 1975 conclude that not only did the Japanese not use the balloons for transmitting biological warfare agents, but the idea had not come up. According to Tanaka, there were no techniques developed for carrying any such agents on balloons in the freezing altitudes that they traveled.

Mark also discovered that of at least 6,000 balloons known to have been launched, 342 were discovered and reported in Alaska, Canada, the United States, and Mexico. Since the war, only thirteen more incidents had been added to the list.

To one way of thinking, this tended to rule out the probability of the professor's suggestion as to how the disease was being spread. Yet when it was considered that the possibility of germ warfare was a factor to those investigating the balloon bombs as far back as 1944 and had been suggested as a possibility, albeit facetiously, by members of Thornesby's staff, it remained a distinct, if remote, chance. Given a more sophisticated system, requiring perhaps a lower altitude, balloons could work. The idea intrigued the Penetrator. He mulled it over as he walked down the broad steps toward the mouth of Jefferson Street, where it dead-ended at First Street in front of the library.

Mark had just entered the pedestrian crossway when he realized he had picked up a tail. Who would be following him and why? He decided to find out. Walking south on First, away from Jefferson and his parked car, the Penetrator felt satisfied to see the pair obediently tagging along. He ducked into the doorway of a small shop and emerged a few seconds later, almost treading on the heels of his pursuers. Their ineptitude was so pathetic it was becoming a game. Mark reversed his course, moving faster now, until he came to the entrance of a service drive between two large stores.

To the two men following the Penetrator, in the confusion resulting from their near encounter with the man they were tailing, it seemed as if he had vanished into thin air. They increased their stride, hurrying now, eyes searching the crowd on both sides of the street. When they reached the drive, the man nearest the building corner suddenly got whisked out of sight.

Chapter 5

OTHER BATTLES

One of Mark's large, powerful hands wrapped around the man's throat, the other grasping his upper right arm. With a strong surge, using the startled tail's momentum, the Penetrator swung him around, slamming the broad back against a brick wall. His head made a satisfying *klonk* against the hard surface, and he sagged as Mark released him, turning to the other man.

"Lars?" asked the unconscious man's companion.

"He's incommunicado right now," the Penetrator told Lars's partner as he jerked the unsuspecting man off his feet. Mark shoved hard, driving wind from suddenly painful lungs. "Now, what the hell is the idea of following me?"

"Hey, take it easy, man. We're federal officers."

"You'll be a crippled federal officer if you don't give me a straight answer."

"In my breast pocket. A card folder. Lars and I are with the U.S. Public Health Service. We were ordered to follow you by our boss."

"Thornesby?"

"That's right, *Dr.* Thornesby. After you interviewed him today he—well, he wanted to find out something more about you. He didn't buy that story of you writing for *Dairy Herd Management*. Thought he knew every writer they had."

The Penetrator released the man, checked his ID; his name was David Colton. "Okay, Dave. So you picked me up outside the library. How did you find me?"

"We're not that far from the office. We decided to cruise the area before starting to look at motels. Dr. Thornesby noticed what car you got into after leaving his office. We spotted it and waited. Listen, from what you were doing, you know, looking up stuff in the library, all that, as far as I can see, you're probably genuine. I mean, that is what writers do, don't they?"

Lars groaned and sat upright, one hand massaging a large lump on the back of his head. "Jeez. What'd you hit me with, fella?"

"A brick wall. Now that I have your undivided attention, I'm going to tell the both of you this just once. What I do and how I choose to do it is nobody's damn business but my own. By now I'd think there were enough tender toes in this incredible bureauracy we're saddled with that the word would be out not to hassle reporters. There is that little thing about freedom of the press, you know."

"All right, all right, I said I'm sorry. He's just a garden variety journalist, right Lars?"

"Fine with me, Dave. But my head hurts like hell."

"Take a refresher course in surveillance, Lars. I made you two before I got five feet from the library steps. Now, I don't care what it is you tell Thornesby, but I want no misunderstanding about this: whatever is said takes you two clowns off my back. You or any others, right?"

Dave shifted his feet, uncomfortable, lips working. "Right," he relented. "We'll cook up something to satisfy the boss."

"I'll count on it. *Adios*, chumps."

By the time Dave Colton had helped Lars to his feet, the Penetrator was lost from sight.

Olaf Swensen's confrontation with the minions of the U.S. Public Health Service wasn't as fortuitous as the Penetrator's. Creighton Thornesby had sent a hand-picked crew of his own henchmen to dispatch Olie's dairy herd. They were men he had personally recruited and used only for killing off uncontaminated herds. With the half a dozen more working on the balloons at the old Bjornsen farm, they constituted Thornesby's entire crew in Wisconsin. The fewer people who knew, the less the risk. They descended on the Swensen farm a little after noon, hard faced, grim, determined to carry out their orders.

"Like hell you're gonna shoot my cows. The state health inspector was here yesterday. He certified the entire herd free of any disease. Pack up and get outta here!"

"We have our orders, Mr. Swensen, and we're going to do what we came here to do."

"Oh, no you won't. I'll get an injunction until I can show the papers to your boss. By God, no one kills this herd. I want your name."

"My name doesn't matter. All you need to know is that I represent the federal government and you'll do what you're told." He turned from Olie's angry retort, ignoring it, ordering his men. "Start blasting them."

"Hold it!" Olie shouted. "You shoot one of my cows, just one, and I'll break your fucking head!"

The blow, when it came, was sudden and unexpected. A rifle butt smacked into Olie's head above one ear, breaking the skin and stunning the powerful athlete's body. Before he could react, another rifle butt was driven deep into his back, over one kidney. Olie sank to his knees, robbed of all ability to resist. A third blow to his forehead blasted into colored lights that faded into darkness.

Johnny Foxkiller and Joey Runningraven had worked for Olie Swensen for five years, since the time his parents had retired and moved into Phillips. Besides being their favorite wide receiver, he was one hell of a fine boss. They looked up to him as an idol. Both boys had dropped out of school at fourteen, and Olie had taken them under his wing, teaching them the dairy business and adding more and more responsibility each year until now they ran the farm alone during the Packers season. When Creighton Thornesby's goon squad turned on Olie and savagely beat him with rifle butts, neither youth wanted to be left out of the action.

Johnny Foxkiller leaped on the back of one rifleman, whipping a wiry arm around his throat and kicking the startled man in the sides. They tumbled to the ground as Joey charged two more, arms flung wide, nails biting deeply into soft flesh as he grasped them in a death hold.

The leader of the slaughter crew rushed to where Johnny and the gunman rolled on the ground. A knife flashed in the Indian boy's free hand, and blood spurted from a long, nasty wound on the foreman's ribs. Two more men, armed with rifles, joined the fray.

The battle, such as it was, ended quickly. But the boot stomping and rifle butt bashing lasted a long time. These men were experts at it, sadists who enjoyed their trade. They left marks that would be permanent on both boys and Olie. Then they started shooting cows.

Kevin Runningraven, Joey's thirteen-year-old

61

brother, had been an unseen witness to the savage brutality of Creighton Thornesby's gunsels. He waited, shaking with anger, until their attention was directed entirely on Olie's herd. Then he broke from cover and started to run. One of the men spotted him and foolishly threw a shot in that direction. It only made the boy run faster.

Kevin stumbled time and again, painfully twisting one ankle, but he made it to State Highway 182. In a few minutes he caught a ride to the junction with State 47, then started a hobbling run the final five miles to the tribal council office on the Lac du Flambeau Reservation. He gasped for breath, head pounding, the country wavering before burning eyes, as he struggled the final thousand yards. With a cry of despair, Kevin fell face forward up the steps.

In minutes word spread through the tribe. Two of their own had been brutally attacked, beaten to bloody messes and, according to the words Kevin tumbled out, were to be taken to the county seat at Phillips and jailed for assaulting federal officers. The young men gathered to speak in angry flashes of rhetoric, each spokesman firing the resolve of the others. The old men of Lac du Flambeau met to discuss this great evil in quiet, slowly thought out discourse.

They were worried, and rightly so. If the fiery voices of the young men were listened to, they could also go as the Menominee had gone. Guns and knives against the white man was a foolhardy path to follow. It would only bring down on them Captain Loyal Nelsen and his SWAT team from Green Bay. It was he who had twice broken the power of the Menominee when they took to the warpath—one man with twelve others to follow him. And that was but a small force, a token, compared to what the federals could bring to bear.

The old men talked long into the afternoon. But by nightfall, war drums throbbed in a nearby copse of birch and cottonwood.

Chapter 6

NEW ALLIES

PACKER STAR END JAILED

Mark Hardin looked at the headline of the *Daily Herald* morning edition with disbelief. Then he quickly read the story below.

Olie Swensen, the article said, was in custody in the Price County Community Hospital at Phillips, charged with resisting federal officers and aggravated assault. A spokesperson for the U.S. Public Health Service had stated that the Swensen herd had been condemned for rampant infection by the unknown disease sweeping the state. Under-Sheriff Gorse of the Prince County Sheriff's office, in reconstructing the incident, indicated that apparently when informed of the condemnation order, Olie Swensen had allegedly attacked the federal men sent to destroy his herd. Joining in the attack, it was alleged, were two Indian employees of Swensen's, John Foxkiller and Joey Runningraven, both of the Lac du

Flambeau Reservation. All three were expected to be released from the hospital later that day to be transferred to the jail. "Some minor force was necessary to subdue them," was the only comment available regarding the suspects' presence in the hospital.

Olie had a temper—Mark knew that only too well from their days playing together for UCLA —but this sort of unreasoning attack on authorities seemed too inconsistent. Mark folded the paper, snapped shut his small clothes bag, and carried all three metal suitcases to his rented Granada. Checking the map, he headed north on U.S. 51 to Healford Junction, where he'd catch U.S. 8 to Patience and turn north to Phillips.

Price County Community Hospital didn't have a jail ward as such, making Mark's entry easier. Judicious altering of one of his many spurious credentials got him past the two sheriff's guards at the door to the room where Olie and his Indian workmen were recovering from their injuries.

As far as the lawmen were concerned, Mark was a representative of the Packers, and it was all right with them for him to visit. Olie was pleasantly surprised to see Mark, but astonished to hear his old friend announced as, "somebody from the team here to see you." He wasted no time in unloading his version of what happened.

"My cows were healthy. I was worried about all this disease talk, so I had the state people come out the day before it happened. They gave the herd a clean bill."

"That's true, mister," Johnny Foxkiller spoke up from the adjoining bed. "There was no reason for those men to do that. Olie showed them the papers."

"Do you still have the papers from the state?"

"I do, if they didn't destroy them to justify what happened."

"That sounds like you believe there's more behind this than a dangerous disease. Some sort of . . . conspiracy?"

"Mark, damnit, I'm not one of these guys who goes around believing every government agency is conspiring to destroy our way of life. That may be true of a few who are off on a power trip. But I've always thought the Public Health Service was meant to help us, not hinder."

"Tell me about these men."

Olie did. Briefly and bitterly, with added details from Johnny and Joey, he described how his herd had come to be slaughtered and how they had wound up in the hospital, charged with federal offenses.

"And they came from Thornesby's office? Under his direct control?"

"That's right." Olie started to say more, but stopped as the door opened. A deputy stood in the opening, orderlies with two gurneys behind him.

"You two," he said, indicating Johnny Fox-killer and Joey Runningraven. "You're to be moved to separate rooms. Orders of the U.S. Attorney." He turned to Mark. "And you can have only two minutes more."

After the transfer was completed, Olie motioned Mark closer to the bed, speaking softly, earnestly. "There's something I don't understand. You came to Wisconsin right after all this started, asked me questions, now you're here. More interrogation, a lot of talk about Creighton Thornesby. Then there's how you got in here. How did you convince them you were with the Packers staff?"

"Never mind that last. Like I told you, Olie, I was in Green Bay on business."

"Yeah. But what sort of business? I don't buy this paper company bull. You work for the government? FBI or CIA, something like that?"

"No. It's like I told you. I'm here for my company, I was curious. Then, when I heard about your trouble, naturally I wanted to do whatever I could."

"Complete with credentials identifying you as part of the PR department of the Packers? C'mon, Mark, don't kid the kidder. It simply doesn't wash. I've played a lot of football, but they haven't battered my brains out entirely. I can add."

"Good for you. But you are in enough trouble as it is. There are simply some things you'd be better off not knowing."

Olie's eyes narrowed, a glint of sudden realization in them. "We get around a lot, the team,

68

you know? Travel, hear things, see a lot of the country and read a lot, you get me? Now, from what's been going on since you arrived, I'm beginning to wonder if your business doesn't involve the use of blue flint arrowheads?"

Mark felt a cold dread filling his belly. There were far too many people who knew he was the Penetrator. Eight in fact. Others had known and they had died, horribly, at the hands of enemies the Penetrator had created over the years, or anonymously without realizing why. Olie knew, or at least suspected enough not to be put off with weak excuses. How could he get out from under? But Olie was going on, pressing his point.

"You're in too good shape to have been pushing napkins or toilet tissue or newsprint for years from behind a desk. And the first time I saw you, you had a bulge in your pocket that could only have been a gun—a little one, but a gun nevertheless. I'll bet you've got one on now. *Paper peddlers don't pack*. Not considered polite in their circles, don't ya know? And you're much too interested in Thornesby and any connection he might have to this mess. So, okay, go get 'em, fella. I won't blow the whistle."

"Olie, I . . . " the Penetrator sighed heavily. "You are too smart for your own good. Look, I didn't come out of the army with the idea of wading through the garbage of this world. I'm not a career do-gooder. It's just that *things* happened and one thing led to another. I'm in up to

69

my eyeballs now, have been for a long time, and no way to extricate myself.

"I can't give myself up to the law. To them I'm a dangerous criminal. They'd put me in prison, and there I wouldn't last a day. Too many men inside there that were put behind bars because of me. If I keep going, I know that some day, somehow, I'll catch a bullet or a knife, or a bomb will scatter little parts and pieces of my car and me all over the countryside. It's inevitable. The thing is, I don't want to take a lot of good friends down with me."

Mark turned from the bed, paced the short way to the window and back. The pale, nausia-green walls of the hospital room failed to perform their supposed function: he was neither calmed nor relaxed. "I don't glory in what I do. I'm merely good at it, damn good. And it seems as equally inescapable that there will be a constant parade of those who prey on the helpless —the parasites, the corrupters whom the law either can't or won't go after.

"Hell, it started a long time ago, back in the army. I got stomped into a bag of jelly by a gang of misfits who thought it was more fun to profit from the black market than fight on the DMZ. I wanted revenge for that, sure, and for . . . something that . . . happened after. But it isn't vengeance that runs me. What I do is something that ought to be done—someone should be doing it. And I, for better or worse, was fool enough to volunteer."

Olie had half raised in his bed, bruised, battered face rigid with rapt attention, peering from white bandages. He sighed softly, wincing as he shook his head. He made a half-gesture with an arm held fast in traction.

"That's heavy, man. *Wheew!* You know something? Most people are for what you do. I mean it. Down inside they know there has to be some alternative to the bleeding heart do-gooders and liberal judges. 'The cops arrest 'em and the judges turn them loose.' You hear it all the time. Sure, there has to be someone standing between the decent people and the animals in the streets; it's the only thing that keeps us nominally civilized. The police used to do that. Now their hands are tied worse than a private citizen's. Then someone like you comes along. Don't think it isn't appreciated—at least by those of us who don't have a vested interest in encouraging crime and making its victims helpless. But there's not a one, I'll bet, for or against you, who realizes the price you have to pay."

Mark changed the subject, embarrassed by the tribute his old friend was paying him. "What I've told you has to be kept absolutely secret. It is information that could get you killed. Don't discuss it with anyone, not even your wife."

"My wife! Jesus! Judy and the kids. She must be frantic."

"I'll look in on her, if you want. I have to go up that way, check into this further. I want to know why Thornesby is having undiseased cows killed off. While I do that, I can let your wife know you are mending and not to worry. Don't you worry, either. If those papers are around, or if the state can produce copies, by the time this is over you'll be out of it free and clear."

"I wish I could be so sure."

Mark grinned. "It's like an Olie Swensen received pass. No sweat to the goal line."

The Penetrator had other worries, however, before he could visit the Swensen farm. An update on the news, on his car radio, informed Mark that feeling was running high at the Lac du Flambeau Reservation. The spirited young men of the tribe were talking about releasing Olie and his two workmen, at gunpoint if necessary. A war dance had been held the previous night. Local authorities were talking about calling in Captain Nelsen and his SWAT team from Green Bay if matters worsened. That was all the Penetrator needed to complicate this affair: an Indian uprising.

## Chapter 7

"You seek the way of honor," the Penetrator told the young men of Lac du Flambeau. "This is right and fit, if done in a sacred manner. But what good is honor received posthumously when the real battles are yet to be fought?"

Mark Hardin and three old men from the tribal council stood in the center of a circle formed by the war dancers. Many of them lay, reclining on one elbow, exhausted from the night's activities. The Penetrator had been introduced to this mixed assemblage of boys, youths, and men in their twenties as a Brother who had fought in the Taos uprising. It assured him a fair hearing.

When the Penetrator had first arrived on the reservation, he wasn't so sure of an opportunity to speak, let alone be listened to seriously. He addressed himself earnestly to the tribal council, in the language of the ancients, the medicine tongue common to most Native Americans from the Rocky Mountains to the Atlantic, from Canada to the tip of South America. It was the common *lingua* of the ancient Polynesian mystics —the *Huna*—and, according to some authorities, it was a degenerated form of spoken Egyptian, as it must have been in the time of the Middle Kingdom. Its effect was immediate and impressive.

The council members broke from their indecisive rambling over the problem facing them and appointed, by vote, Mark as their spokesman to the war faction and took him to the copse to introduce him. There was sullen suspicion and resentment among many of the warriors, but no open hostility. When Mark began, he first lighted the tribal pipe, presenting it to the six powers in the proper sequence, then held it before him at arm's length, turning constantly so that all in the circle could hear and see him. Gradually the gap closed in their divergent thinking.

"Our Brothers, Foxkiller and Runningraven, have been arrested by the white police. Getting them out by force would only add to the legal problems. There are papers I was told about that will prove the federal men acted illegally. I'm going to the Swensen farm now to get those papers. With them, it can be proven that Olaf and our Brothers acted in self-defense and in defense of Olaf's herd. They will have to be freed. By tomorrow everyone should be home."

There were grunts and shouts of approval;

several men slapped a bare thigh as a sign of approbation. The smaller boys gave a ragged cheer, "*Hé-aaah, hé-aaah, hé-aaah!*"

Many of the would-be war party left the circle, staggering with fatigue, heading to their homes to sleep. For the time being, the Penetrator had averted a development that could only prove tragic.

As the white-coated figure approached the doorway, Deputy Claasen of the Price County Sheriff's Department sat upright in his chair, raising one hand to stop the newcomer. "Sorry, the man in this room is in custody. No one permitted in except the doctor assigned to the case, the U.S. Attorney, and his own lawyer, of course."

"I'm Dr. Creighton Thornesby, U.S. Public Health Service. Mr. Swensen's herd was destroyed yesterday due to contamination. After the death of Karl Kruger, that farmer from Rhinelander, it is essential I have blood samples, make some other tests on Olaf Swensen, a John Foxkiller and Joey Runningraven. We must know if they have been infected also."

Claasen blanched. "Sure. Go on in, Doctor. Do whatever you have to. I wouldn't want that stuff loose around me. The other two are right down the hall, 209 and 214. Sure hope they don't have it."

Smiling, one hand inside a coat pocket, fingers

75

fondling a small phial, Creighton Thornesby entered Olie Swenson's room.

Mark accepted thanks from the council and gracefully declined offers of help from both them and the young men of the tribe. He could, he told them, easily carry a handful of papers back to the U.S. Attorney and see that the arrested men were released. Kevin Runningraven gave Mark detailed directions to the Swensen farm, and he drove away.

Half an hour later, Mark stopped the Granada in the empty farmyard at Olie's home. A shaggy collie barked fitfully from inside the fenced lawn of the two-story Georgian farmhouse. Nothing else stirred until Mark stepped onto the ground. From the corner of his eye, he noted the flicker of a window curtain. A few moments later the back door opened a crack.

"Who are you? What do you want?" a woman's voice asked tentatively. Although nothing could be seen of her, the muzzle and some ten inches of the blue steel barrel of the 12 gauge shotgun she held were clearly visible.

"Judy Swensen? I'm a friend of your husband. We played football together at UCLA."

"My husband doesn't have any friends. He's in jail."

"No, he's not. He's in the hospital. I just came from seeing him some four hours ago." The Penetrator stopped. It was obvious she didn't believe him, the shotgun pointed directly at him now, a black *O* of death. Using his cover name would mean nothing, gain him only more suspicion from Judy Swensen, and possibly push her over the edge of endurance. He didn't want to use his own name, but reluctantly he realized it was the only way.

"Listen to me carefully. *I am Mark Hardin.* Olie said he had told you about me. We were roommates for a while at the Lambda Chi house. We both played first string for UCLA in '65 and '66."

"Mark?" Judy asked disbelievingly. Then, with a flood of relief that turned to dry, weary sobs, "Oh, Mark."

The shotgun muzzle wavered, lowered to point at the porch floor, and the door swung open. Judy Swensen stepped out onto the screened-in porch, holding open the outer door. Mark walked up to the steps.

"You'll have to forgive me. I—I haven't been myself since . . . it happened." She tried a shy, incomplete smile.

"That's more like it. May I come in?"

Inside the kitchen two small boys with cotton-white hair sat at the table, interrupted in the midst of peanut butter sandwiches and large glasses of milk. Their large, china-blue eyes widened in solemn concentration as they gazed at the stranger who had entered.

"Tommy and Nils," Judy made the introductions. "And this is Mr. Hardin, a friend of Daddy's. Sit down, Mark." She brushed at a blonde lock that had fallen from her tied-back hair.

"I know this has been a tough go for you all. I happened to be in the area, and when I heard what had gone on, I offered Olie any help I could give."

"It's appreciated, believe me. But what can be done?" Her normally pretty features were drawn with tension, gray eyes dulled by defeat.

"Olie mentioned some papers the state inspector had given him. Do you have them?"

"Why, yes. But what good are they now? The cows are all dead, and Olie's going—going to jail." Her eyes filled with tears.

"Not if we can prove that the herd was healthy and that he acted to protect his property from unlawful destruction. The prosecution will have to prove that Olie and his workmen had guilty knowledge and committed a willful attack on federal officers while they were in lawful pursuit of their duties. The federal health people claim there is a seven- to fourteen-day incubation period for the infection. If we can show, through these state examiners' certificates, that the cows were healthy within twenty-four hours of the time Thornesby's men shot them, the case against Olie falls apart."

Judy's eyes cleared, sparkling with renewed promise, but her mouth tightened. She was afraid to hope, and her words were a challenge. "Are you an attorney?"

"No. But I have a good one, and I can have

him here inside a day if we need him. What would help more is to have blood tests now, two days after that state report, showing that your cows were still not contaminated."

"How? They're all dead. Those men brought in bulldozers, dug big holes and pushed in the cattle, covered them up." The despair was starting to return, tears making silent, slick trails down Judy's cheeks. She lowered her head to her hands.

"Mom—Mommy," Tommy, the eldest at nine, started haltingly. "The—there is a way. The calves. Remember?"

Judy looked up, hope rekindling. "I don't know what's the matter with me. Why didn't I think? Of course. The calves. I'm sorry, Mark, I just don't seem to be functioning on all cylinders since yesterday when they . . . to—took Olie away."

The thing is, we do have a chance now. Tell me about the calves, Tommy."

"I . . . hid them. Yesterday when those men came. They were to be my Four-H project, and I was afraid for them. But they're only babies."

"Three days old yesterday," Judy took up the tale. "They were still on suck. So, if the milk was contaminated, they would be too. Oh, Mark will it really help?"

"Bet on it. I have, ah, some things in the car to take samples with. It would be nice to get blood samples, urine specimens from each of you, too. Prove that no persons or animals on this

79

farm were contaminated. I'm not sure what the lab would need, but chances are those would do."

"That's marvelous, Mark. I'm actually beginning to believe there's a way out for us. We—we could make the government pay for our herd if we proved there was nothing wrong with them, couldn't we?"

"I'm fairly sure you could. Now, where is the nearest state agricultural station?"

"In Wausau."

"Good. I'll be heading back there after I'm through here anyway. I'll go get things ready. You finish that peanut butter sandwich, Tommy, then come show me those calves."

An hour later, the Penetrator had secured all the samples he needed, wrapped them in a small box, and placed them in the refrigerator until he was ready to leave. Then he turned to a task, vital if Olie intended to restock, that had been unfulfilled because of the beating and arrest of the Packers star. All of the corrals, feed bunks, stock barns, and the milk barn had to be sprayed with a powerful disinfecting solution left at the farm by Thornesby's men.

Emptying a five-gallon container of the concentrate into the white cylinder of Olie's sprayer and leaving it to fill by hose from an outside faucet near the main barn, he went to the equipment shed to get a small tractor, which he brought back and attached to the spraying rig. When the tank was filled, Mark drove into the first corral, manually lowered the spindly-looking spray booms, and climbed back on the tractor. Engaging the power-takeoff, he shifted gears, tapped the throttle open a little further, and started on his rounds. It was necessary to spray everything once, allowing it to set twenty-four hours; then the corrals were to be scraped to dry ground, disinfected again, and left for a week before restocking could be done.

Combined with treating the buildings, it was more work than the Penetrator had time for, and he made a mental note to contact the reservation. He would ask for volunteers among the young men. The hard work would help them boil off their anger. As he drove in narrowing circles, Mark added up what he knew so far. Each run-through wound up in the same place. Thornesby.

Acting and speaking in the name of the forces of good, Creighton Thornesby, the Penetrator became convinced, seemed to do nothing but bad. Who were the members of this special killer squad? They didn't act in accordance with everything Mark knew about the U.S. Public Health Service. Proof of Olie's herd being free of contamination would go a long way toward jarring loose some answers. Meanwhile, he had a lot of work to do.

In three hours Mark had treated all three main corrals, the feed bunks, wash yard, and milking barn. He parked the tractor and started working on foot in the first of four large stock barns with

81

a backpack tank sprayer. As he progressed, a sudden, piercing wail came from the house. It was followed by the sounds of unremitting anguish. He slipped from the straps of the portable sprayer and ran to the back door.

"Oh, nooo. No, no, no. Ooooh, God, no. Not Olie," Judy Swensen moaned in hysterical grief. She sat on the floor, slumped against one wall, hands covering her face, rocking back and forth from time to time as she repeated the words over and over. Beside her shoulder the handset of the telephone dangled, spinning slightly.

"Judy, what is it?" the Penetrator snapped firmly.

"Olie . . . Olie. Oh, my dear God, my Olie!"

She was beyond rational answers. A faint buzz of voice came from the phone. Mark bent to retrieve it. "Hello. This is a friend of the Swensens. What the hell did you tell this woman? She's gone hysterical."

"I . . . why . . . we . . . that is, this is Price County Community Hospital. I only called to inform Mrs. Swensen that her husband has just passed away from the infectious disease that is attacking the dairy herds."

"Thanks a whole hell of a lot, lady. You have such a tactful manner about you," Mark rasped. Then he gained command again, refusing to believe what he knew could not be. "That's impossible. I saw him just this morning."

"All the same, he is dead."

"Who's been in to see him since I was there?"

There came a hesitation on the far end of the line. Mark put harsh authority into his voice, covering with forced anger the bitter feelings of grief and guilt he had for leaving Olie unprotected. "I'm with the PR department of the Packers, nurse. I'd better get an answer."

"No one, sir. Only Dr. Thornesby of Public Health. He was in about three hours after you left. He also certified the cause of death. I—I'm sorry. We—all of us in Price County thought of Olie as a local hero. I'm terribly sorry." There was a hint of tears in the young woman's voice.

"Thank you, nurse. I understand. Are you sure that only Dr. Creighton Thornesby and no one else entered Olie Swensen's room?"

"Yes, sir."

"Thank you." Mark hung up and bent to lift Judy to her feet. She was like a limp clothes dummy, completely without volition of her own. He guided her to a chair in the living room, got her a cup of hot coffee and a stiff three fingers of bourbon from a bottle on a high shelf.

"Drink this."

"No. I don't want it. Nothing . . . nothing in this world matters now. Our farm is ruined, my husband is dead, my children are fatherless. Why? For the love of God, why?"

"Drink," Mark commanded harshly, pressing the glass of whiskey to her lips. She swallowed, choked, swallowed again, and reached for the coffee.

"Dry your eyes, Judy. You have two hurt,

grieving little boys to comfort. They need you. Help them and yourself."

Judy Swensen gulped back more tears, dabbed at her eyes, then emptied the coffee cup with one long swallow. Fussing with her hair, she stood, somewhat unsteadily. "Where—where are they?"

"Nils is upstairs. I don't know where Tommy is."

Nils Swenson sat on his bed, dry-eyed, a look of disbelief and forlorn agony on his face. His lips twisted with the effort of saying the words. "Daddy isn't . . . dead, Mom. Please, Mommy, say Daddy isn't dead." Judy rushed to her son, and they had a cry together while Mark went in search of Tommy.

He found the boy in the hayloft of the largest barn. Tommy's face was puffy, eyes red rimmed and swollen. Choking gasps held back more tears. The Penetrator found he had no words to offer, neither consolation nor hope. He had run out, for the moment, of that strength that is needed to bolster those consumed with grief. His own eyes watered and spilled over, wetting his cheeks. Without speaking, Mark led the boy, hand in hand, back to his mother. After making arrangements for someone to come be with Judy, he left, taking the samples and papers, heading for Wausau.

Thornesby, the Penetrator thought as he roared south down the main road. It was Thornesby who had condemned first Kruger's cows and then Olie's. Now both men were dead. Thornesby had

84

condoned the brutal brutal beating Olie received, seen to his hospitalization, and charged him with crimes against the government. Thornesby again who had visited Olie that morning and, once more, Thornesby who had signed the death certificate stating that Olie had died of a disease he could not possibly have caught from his cows, who didn't have it in the first place. Be-nice time was over for Creighton Thornesby, the Penetrator grimly vowed.

No more go-easy approach to the Public Health Service doctor. There was a glint in the Penetrator's eye that few men ever saw and lived to talk about. It was time for a more direct approach to Dr. Creighton Thornesby, and the Penetrator looked forward to it with growing anticipation.

Chapter 8

CAPTIVE

There was a phone message for Mark when he returned to his motel in Wausau after leaving the samples and inspection forms off at the state agriculture office. He checked the number; it was one of several made-up sequences that indicated a real telephone number he was to call. In his room, he connected with the Stronghold and attached his scrambler.

"There have been some new developments in this matter, my boy. I was sure you would like to know right away."

"We've had a few developments of our own," Mark replied, and told Professor Haskins about Olie's death.

"Seems it might fit in with what I have. First, the body of Karl Kruger was found near one of several farms owned by a Theophilus Wen. According to the computer, Wen is part of a multinational conglomerate. Through various front men, Wen's corporate entity has been buying up farms in the stricken area. Also anything else they can get their hands on: small cheese companies, milk-processing plants, those sorts of businesses. You have no doubt already guessed that this multinational conglomerate is the same one Creighton Thornesby has large stock holdings in." The Penetrator whistled softly into the phone.

"You might be interested in this, too," Professor Haskins went on. "Theophilus Wen is suspected of being part of a radical, elitist cabal. One made up of survivors of the *Société Internationale d'Elite.*"

"I thought Wo Fat Ling was the only one of importance who escaped from that mess."

"Apparently not, Mark. It seems there were a great number of smaller fry, along with a few big fish, who slipped through the Justice Department's net. If I may be allowed to carry that trite simile a little further, the government was more interested in who they had physically in custody than in those who got away. They spent their time checking to see if any Red herring or Chinese carp were mixed into the bouillabaisse."

The Penetrator was in no mood for levity after the death of his friend and the grieving family he had left outside Fifield. "Save the jokes to tell to the computer. Let's get on with it."

"I'm sorry, Mark. After what's happened, I shouldn't have tried to be funny. It was thoughtless of me. Unforgivable. Anyway, Wen is one of this new elitist, One-Worlder gang. He and Thornesby are connected through mutual business interests. Perhaps Thornesby could have been in SIE? They did have their tentacles into the military, as you should well know."

"That they did, but their major thrust was after generals and Pentagon types, field grade officers and above. Civilian employees, even at Dougway, would be hard to approach. I like the connection, though, Professor. Any more?"

"That's all at this time."

Mark asked for detailed directions to the Wen farm. It had originally belonged to a family named Bjornsen, who had sold out six months prior, retired, and moved to Tomahawk. After he hung up, the Penetrator armed himself lightly with his derringers, a Mark IV, Colt .45 auto in his snug-fitting Pancake holster, and a pair of night glasses. He planned a soft probe of this farm; then, using the intelligence gathered, he intended to be ready to strike hard at Thornesby and his cabalistic friend, Theophilus Wen.

The Penetrator parked his Granada half a mile from the Wen farm, then moved in for a close look. Using shallow gullies and scattered stands of birch, hickory, and cottonwood, he worked his way to within a hundred yards of the old dairy. His night glasses gave a clear view of the farmyard. No sign of life showed around the house or most of the outbuildings. The light-gathering capabilities of the special binoculars did reveal sliver-thin bars of brightness here and there from one large barn. The Penetrator revised his plan, centering his probe on the only source of activity.

Patience was rewarded within fifteen minutes as Mark noted a slight movement to one side of the yard. A man stealthily crossed from one structure to the next—a guard, obviously. Now the Penetrator had the problem of timing the man—determining his route so as to be able to slip past him and learn what went on in the barn, or else deciding to take out the man, thus risking discovery of his visit and losing the element of surprise. Moments later he made his decision.

The man stopped abruptly, stepping into the open front of an equipment shed. A flame, from a cigarette lighter, burgeoned into a blossom of blue-outlined orange in the night glasses. He inhaled deeply, exhaled a cloud of smoke, then turned, his shoulders hunching in the characteristic posture of a man relieving himself. While he was occupied at this task, the Penetrator sprang to his feet, dashing noiselessly on soft-soled moccasins to a point well inside the patrolled area.

Cautiously the Penetrator worked himself from the deep shadow of one building to another, from storage bin to chicken house, until he crouched against one outside wall of the barn. The guard, his cigarette finished, resumed patrol again, attention directed outward, seeking signs of a possible intrusion. Not once did his gaze appear to check the area of the barn. The Penetrator watched him for five minutes, confident then that the guard's sphere of responsibility lay elsewhere and his own successful infiltration had gone unnoticed.

A side door, outlined by vertical and horizontal slashes of brightness, stood only a few feet from where Mark waited. He moved toward it with care, checking to avoid protruding nails, old boards and loose gravel. Voices, muffled and indistinct, came from inside and, placing an ear to a crack, the Penetrator heard them resolve faintly into a conversation between three men.

"I still think the Doc's nuts ordering another release tonight. I'm not sure the weather's gonna hold. There's a front moving in, thunderstorms brewing. We could have the whole batch pushed out over Lake Michigan and dumped in the water. But that's just the least of our worries. That thing with the football player's gonna make all hell break loose."

"You've got a point there, Hal."

"Sure I do, Ed. You can bet those last few hairs on that balding pate of yours that the stink from this one will bring in more law than we can cope with. Hell, it wouldn't surprise me if the Air Force got into the act, chasin' down the balloons."

The third man spoke up. "Hal, Ed. Look at the bright side. How does anyone know we're using balloons? For that matter, how would anybody be aware that this disease wasn't natural in the first place?"

"Look who's turned optimist—Ton-of-Fun Turner."

"Fat men are supposed to be jolly, right, Ed? Look, Hal, we know what's going on, and Doc Thornesby sure as hell is aware of it. But anyone else who has ever suspected anything at all is with us or dead. Why sweat it? Let's just do our job and let it go at that."

"I'll tell you how," Hal growled. "We know that not all the balloons we've launched have been accounted for. Places we planned for the disease to break out, it hasn't. Other areas, where the flight plan didn't call for it, got saturated. Once we turn those balloons loose, there's nothing to guide them but the winds. They could go anywhere. And there's nothing to make them find cows and squirt bacteria directly on them.

"They coulda popped over Lake Michigan, like I said before, or hit a cross-wind and blown clear the hell and gone to Canada, maybe even the Arctic Circle. Polar bears don't get sick from it."

"Okay. I'll go along with that. But what says the strays tell anyone balloons are being used to spread the disease?"

"Use your head, Turner. If all that could happen, isn't it possible one or more of the balloons came down intact—that maybe right now someone in the FBI lab or some cop in Podunk Junction isn't sitting at a desk trying to figure out what the balloons were being used for and who might have sent them up?"

"I'm not so sure of that, Hal," Ed countered

his associate. "Doc Thornesby said that the chances of anyone being even remotely curious about a burst meteorology balloon were almost nil."

"Speaking of the Doc, where is he? He should've been here by now. We're short handed as it is, and he's never missed a launch yet."

"He could have been delayed," the optimistic Turner offered. "This thing with taking off the Swensen guy could easily louse up Doc's schedule."

"Yeah. So we do a solo performance, men. Let's hop to it," Hal ordered.

The Penetrator had heard enough. His major concern had shifted from *why* Thornesby and his men were doing what they did, to stopping them from doing it again. This place had to be destroyed and along with it the deadly bacteria the lab technicians were releasing in balloons. Thornesby might not be here, but he could be tracked down, and then the Penetrator would have the answers to the whys. Now he had to get to his motel, select the materials for his blitz, and return undetected. Planning his moves, Mark started for the far corner of the barn.

Mark had taken only two steps when a command was barked: "Freeze!"

Chapter 9

ABRUPT DEPARTURE

The voice came from the darkness beyond the barn.

"Hands behind your head and walk back to that door."

Instinct, hunch, perhaps even the end of shift, the Penetrator realized with sinking feeling, something had caused the guard to break his normal routine and take a swing past the barn. The man stood too far away for the Penetrator to take a chance jumping the shotgun. He was caught. He had no choice but to comply.

"Now, open the door and step through."

"How can I do that with my hands up?"

"Left hand. And make it slow. Move!"

Their exchange had attracted attention from inside. Hal and his companions burst suddenly through the door, surrounding Mark, getting in the line of fire from the guard. In an instant the advantage had shifted to the Penetrator.

"What's going on out here, Randy?" Hal asked a second before he was seized by the Penetrator and hurled toward the guard. Hal was short and slim, with a Hilter moustache and rimless glasses. He must have weighed no more than 130 pounds. As such, he made an excellent missile.

Hal's bony chest slammed into Randy, the guard. The shotgun blasted sharply into the night. Both men received flash and powder burns from the muzzle, but the shot column slashed into the eaves and wall of the barn. The Penetrator wasn't taking time for critical evaluations, though. He had already turned on Ed, jerking the startled lab technician toward him as one fist smashed at Ed's face.

A heavy body hurtled toward Mark as Turner plowed into the Penetrator's legs, bowling him off his feet. Then Hal and Ed were on top of Mark, punching, wrestling to get a pinning hold. The Penetrator managed a gouge at a nerve under the base of Ed's chin, loosening his grip. Mark brought up a knee, dumping fish-smelling breath from Ed's lungs as Mark connected. Ed fell away and the Penetrator turned his concentration to Hal, whose flailing fists were pounding him on the face and neck.

"Hold him still, hold him still!" Randy shouted. Then he took three swift strides, standing over the writhing mass, shotgun held with the buttplate downward. As he saw his target clearly, Randy drove the clubbed weapon toward the Penetrator's forehead.

Mark saw the blow coming and jerked to one side. He managed to miss the full impact, but it stunned him, all strength and conscious control leaving his arms and legs. Quickly the four men fell upon him, rolling Mark over and trussing him like a pilfered pig. They carried him inside and dumped him in a corner of the barn.

They searched Mark, removing his .45, sleeve knife, and High Standard derringers. "My God," Randy said, "this guy's a walking arsenal. You think he's a cop?"

"Could be. Yeah, he probably is," Hal amended. "I don't know of any normal guy who'd walk around with more'n one gun on."

"Then the shit's really gonna hit the fan," Ed added. "We'd better kill him right now."

"Later. We can do whatever's necessary after we finish. First we have to get this launch completed and contact Thornesby if he isn't here before we're through. We'll have to move the entire operation."

"You're telling me? Hal, I say we oughta kill this cop right now. He's seen us, knows what's going on."

"Work first. It's not our decision to make. Now get on it!"

Groggy, but not unconscious, his head aching like an aggregate national skull on New Year's Day, the Penetrator was able to watch while the three men went about their tasks, Randy having gone back on guard. Quickly Mark put together the entire vicious scheme.

Stacked the length of one wall and across the back end of the barn were olive drab painted crates, their military markings still on them, identifying their contents as weather balloons. A compressor and helium-generating plant that were apparently well used occupied one corner. Dust and cobwebs hung from the bare rafters, but where Hal and his coworkers were filling a balloon, the area had been meticulously cleared. With a light shift, there was no one to watch the Penetrator continuously, and Mark took full advantage of his enemy's weakness.

Working cautiously, with a minimum of telltale movement, Mark slid the buckle of his belt around to the rear, where his hands were tied. He had loosened and resewn the belt loops of his trousers so that they were attached by only a pair of thin threads. They broke easily with a firm tug, allowing the thick leather belt to slide freely.

As carefully as he had been searched by Hal and Randy, the Penetrator had two weapons remaining. In addition to a piano wire garrote, five folded hundred-dollar bills, and a wire-saw contained in a flat zippered compartment on the inside of his belt, Mark also had the leather band itself, a Protecto-Belt, made by Bingham, Ltd. in Georgia. The buckle of this unusual survival weapon detached from what appeared to be a solid clasp and revealed itself to be a palm knife, with a triangular blade and curved hilt that fit comfortably in the hand to make a formidable "push" weapon. Freed of its leathery hiding place, it would have been immediately recognizable to Mark's Native American ancestors.

Similar push-knife weapons were familiar to the Cherokee, Seneca, Powhatan, and Kikapoo of the North and to the Aztec, Maya, and Inca of the Southern hemisphere. Mark had first seen a modern one several months ago at the Yuma, Arizona, gun show. His appreciation of the deadly hidden tool was immediate.

Mark ordered one at the Bingham booth, operated personally by knife designer and arms dealer, Sandy Brygider. The Protecto-Belt was only one survival accessory manufactured by his company. Mark had filled out an order form, using a cover name and dead-drop mail address, then paid for his purchase in cash. He looked over the other items in the display and covertly evaluated the man he had dealt with.

Although his posture was outwardly diffident, Sandy gave the impression of a powerful, aggressive nature. He was a normal looking six-foot, 175-pound, blue-eyed fellow, with neatly trimmed brown hair and broad shoulders, definitely not one who would stand out in a crowd. But his eyes were quick, never missing anything that happened around him. He'd make a powerful and dangerous opponent, the Penetrator thought, or a damn fine friend.

Sandy extended a hand, thanking Mark for his purchase. His grip was firm, as hard as the Penetrator's, and his voice had an intense level that convinced the Penetrator that Sandy was truly interested in the answers to questions he asked. Under other, more normal circumstances, Mark felt the man would prove a good ally, both valued and valuable. The usefulness of Sandy's hidden weapon, however, was about to have its first serious field application.

Mark dislodged it and set to work slicing through his bonds. When the Protecto-Belt had arrived at the deep-cover post office box of Paul Lewis, the Penetrator had honed its twin edges to hair-splitting sharpness. With the edges done to surgical perfection, Mark had found it necessary to add an inner lining of latigo leather to reinforce the scabbard. He had done the same thing to the tip end of the belt to strengthen the clasp holes. He could exert exceptional effort now without a mishap that might reveal the belt's secrets. Sharp steel made short work of the thin nylon cord that bound him, and the Penetrator bent to cut free his legs.

On his feet, Mark crouched low to keep in the shadows thrown by a single incandescent bulb hanging over the workbench. He searched his pockets for any object that might aid his immediate problem. Somehow he had to destroy this place. To smash the equipment and render Thornesby's maniacal scheme inoperative was his objective. The hardest part would be eliminating the bacterial agent they were using. It should be sterilized or, better still, consumed in flame. His searching hand uncovered a paper match book. A trip back to Wausau might not be necessary. He could send the whole place up in smoke.

Quickly gathering together what he could find for kindling, the Penetrator built a fire. Shielding the flare from observation with his body, Mark struck two matches at once and touched them to the shredded paper packing materials and slivers of wood. A feeble flame wavered for a few seconds, then caught and bloomed bigger. Mark added some larger wood from a packing case, nodded in satisfaction, and turned to make his escape.

"Hey, Ed, better check that dude back there. He seems too quiet for my liking."

"Sure, Hal."

The Penetrator left his fire scene in time to come face to face with Ed, who was intent on finding him. The Protecto-Belt knife was in Mark's hand in "push" fashion, blade extended between two middle knuckles, hilt firmly against Mark's palm. He thrust out and upward before Ed could register alarm or surprise.

The needle tip slid into Ed's stomach just below the rib cage, angling upward, piercing the diaphragm and shearing open the bottom of the unfortunate lab technician's heart. Ed gave a soft *whumph* and fell to the floor, dead of shock and massive internal hemorrhage. Mark fished a pair of flint arrowheads from his belt pocket and tossed them into the lighted area. By then the flames had grown to ceiling height, crackling and eating into the ancient, dry-rot-infested wood.

Hal spotted it as the Penetrator cleared the door, running toward his car.

"Hey! Fire! Grab an extinguisher. Ed, what the hell's going on back there? Ed?"

Chapter 10

MIDNIGHT MOVE

As Hal, Turner, and Randy frantically fought the fire, the Penetrator put distance between him and his former captors. Halfway through a pasture, he stopped to look back on the results of his efforts.

Flames leaped through the loft now, eating in orange deliverance at the edges of the ancient shingles on the peaked roof. The two lab men realized now that they were incapable of halting the blaze and turned to rescuing their equipment, aided by the outside guard. While the Penetrator observed them, they were able to save the helium-generating plant, several cases of balloons, and a refrigerator chest that undoubtedly contained phials of dormant bacteria. As rafters and floor joists crashed inward in showers of orange and crimson sparks, the men set to dragging their salvaged materials farther from the conflagration.

As the Penetrator watched the collapse of the

barn, headlights appeared on the road to the east of the farm. The car accelerated suddenly when it was near enough for the occupants to have seen the source of the fire. That would be Thornesby, the Penetrator reasoned. Burnt out of his base of operations, Thornesby would have to do something about it. That left no time for a trip to Wausau and back. Stripped of his arms, save the dimunitive blade from his Protecto-Belt and a garrote, Mark couldn't make an end of it now. All he could do was hang loose and see what developed.

"What sort of careless stupidity brought this on?" Creighton Thornesby demanded as he hurriedly left his car. He was shaking with anger and worry.

Hal undertook to explain. "We—we had a prisoner, Doctor. Some cop snooping around here. He got loose and musta set the fire to cover his escape."

"A policeman? What did he look like?"

Hal described the Penetrator.

"That's him!" Thornesby shouted. "That nosy reporter who was snooping around the office this morning. A cop! I knew there was something phony about him. But how did he get on to this place, and what was he doing here?"

Hal extended his hand, opening it to reveal twin blue flint arrowheads about two inches long. "He knifed Ed and threw these at us as he ran out the door."

Theophilus Wen, Thornesby's passenger, had left the car and come up beside the others. He took one look at the objects in Hal's hand and spoke with bitterness, tinged with fear. "The Penetrator."

"What?"

"Somehow, Creighton, the Penetrator has caught on to our operation. We'll have to move to another location quickly, before he comes back to finish what he started."

"But what have these arrowheads to do with the Penetrator?"

"I don't know. I don't imagine anyone is sure of exactly what they mean. But every time the Penetrator mixes into something, one or more of them show up."

The hand-shaped stone points had first appeared in Las Vegas, when Mark had declared war on the Pink Pussy. He had employed them as a terror weapon to help shake loose information by making those who worked for her feel that there was someone to fear more than the Fraülein. It had worked, and from that time on the Penetrator had used the blue flint arrowheads to mark his passage through society's gutters. It was like counting coups, David Red Eagle suggested. In the olden days a warrior frequently fought alone, on a challenge, or emerged from battle the sole survivor of a small band of friends. In such a case he would leave behind some distinctive item of clothing or decoration that would signify to all who saw it who it was that had been victorious. Its modern application was soon noted and commented upon by criminals and the press alike. The ancient weapon quickly became the symbol of Penetrator vengeance.

Theophilus Wen had ample opportunity to be familiar with the Penetrator's trademark. He had been one of seven men to escape from the front of the Maryland Country Club, where SIE had its headquarters, on that chilly, foggy morning when the Penetrator launched his final, devastating attack. As the sleek black Lincoln sped toward Washington, D.C., the men had vowed to rescue what resources they could and offer a reward for the Penetrator—dead. It was a contract, plain and simple, but only one of several put out by crime lords at home and abroad. Rarely had anyone attempted to collect the nearly $3/4 million in bounty money out on the Penetrator. And among those who tried, none so far had lived to explain why they had failed.

This fact alone was enough to account for Theophilus Wen's ashen features and inner disquiet. He spoke to Hal and the others, the ruddy glow of the dying fire turning his pale face an incongruous baby pink.

"We'll have to get this out of here fast. I'll use the radio phone to locate another truck. Start loading and covering the critical items before the local fire department arrives."

"If they ever do," Creighton Thornesby spoke calmly. "It's a volunteer outfit and some distance from here. There isn't another occupied house within four miles. This late at night I doubt if anyone has seen this and called it in. We're certainly not going to report it. Get busy men; the cold in that fridge will last only a few hours, and we want it plugged in long before that."

"Where will you go?" Wen asked.

"That other place of yours, over closer to Rhinelander."

"Sounds good. Remember, that money will be in here tomorrow. We can't afford a prying investigation around that $475,000 or near the balloons. Then there's the Penetrator. Once he starts in on something, he doesn't let go until he's satisfied it is smashed. We'll have to dig in, and you should maintain a very low profile."

"I've been thinking about that. I'll notify the office that I'll be in the field indefinitely. I was going to do it anyway, in connection with Phase Two, but that would have been next week."

Hal returned from an open front shed, driving a one-ton truck. He stopped near the salvaged equipment and walked to where the others stood. Behind him, Randy and Turner wrestled the apartment-size refrigerator into the truck bed.

"I forgot to mention, Doc, that this Penetrator guy hasn't any guns. We took them away from him."

"That means he'll head for a new supply," Wen reckoned aloud.

"So. We have time to make the transfer in peace. At least no one can be watching us now."

Chapter 11

SATURATION TECHNIQUE

Creighton Thornesby's optimistic evaluation of their situation erred on the side of ignorance. Other eyes indeed watched them—those of the Penetrator.

It could be excused of Thornesby, who had known nothing of the Penetrator until informed by his partner in crime. Theophilus Wen, despite his previous shattering experience with the Penetrator's methods, could even be forgiven a momentary lapse when faced with the fiery evidence of the presence of his nemesis. Yet such justification would comfort them little if they knew how close retribution lay.

From twenty yards out in the darkness, Mark Hardin watched as the lab technicians dismantled the helium-generating plant and stowed it aboard the truck. They completed their task as another rig entered the drive. Hal and his men quickly loaded the first vehicle with the remaining loose items, and it departed while the second was loaded with cases of meteorology balloons. The Penetrator had seen what he'd stayed for—and he had a bonus. Four-hundred-thousand dollars. Perhaps he could find some way to turn all that money to his own use.

Hurrying to the Granada, Mark drove without lights to a point where he could watch for the departure of the second truck. He cursed what he called his momentary lapse of sanity, which had caused him to come prepared for only a soft probe. All his other weaponry remained behind at the Exel Inn in Wausau. He could only tag along, learn all he could, and make his final move hours later. But then, being captured hadn't been in his plans, nor having to burn his way to freedom. With the enemy alerted, he would have to content himself with a mobile recon.

The other truck was moving now, turning onto the road in the direction taken by the previous vehicle. Mark eased forward, keeping a loose tail, lights out. Both hands on the wheel, the Penetrator maintained a leisurely pace along arrow-straight country roads that seemed to cross and recross the sinuous course of the Flambeau river. Avoiding all towns, the dust trail of the truck led Mark eastward toward the small community of Rhinelander. At last the distant tail lights swung into a narrow, rutted dirt drive.

The Penetrator stopped far short of the farm lane and slipped quietly from the car. He had taken the precaution of removing the fuses for the convenience lights, so that no sudden brightness would betray his presence. What he needed was a weapon, any kind of weapon. In that long-ago conversation Mark had held with Sandy Brygider, mention had been made by the arms man of a conversion unit for M-16 rifles that allowed them to fire .22 long rifle ammunition and be fully silenced. How handy that cheap-to-fire, light-to-carry Atchisson Mark II Converter modification would be now, Mark thought. He would, he glumly conceded, even welcome a bolt-action shotgun at that moment. Salvaged balloons full of buckshot holes wouldn't fly too well. Such speculation was useless. The Penetrator moved in closer to learn what more he could.

Other men had arrived, members of Thornesby's special animal slaughter crew. In the confusion of setting up the new plant, no effort was being made toward a perimeter guard. Mark was able to slip in close to the rear of a battered barn that sagged on its crumbling foundation at the edge of a clump of birch saplings. From that vantage point, he clearly heard the discussion going on inside.

"I've been giving it some thought while we were driving over here, Theo. If the Penetrator is as bad medicine as you say he is, we should accelerate the program."

"I don't know, Creighton. Speeding up these land purchases might cause undue attention."

"Undue attention! What the hell do you call being burned out of our base of operations? At the least I'm going to launch Phase Two immediately instead of waiting a week."

"Don't you feel you are being premature? There's been no groundwork laid."

"On the contrary, Theo. Phase Two involves a nonlethal viral agent that will cause a rare form of influenza to spread all over the country. As for preparing the public, the swine flu scares of the past years and that Legionnaire's disease thing back in '76 and '77 are ideal background. Once the first few cases are spotted—the farther apart the better—it won't take long to convince everyone there is a dangerous national epidemic. Given a week of that, the public will be ripe for our non-existent right-wing extremist group's ultimatum."

There was a hint of madness in Crighton Thornesby's calm-sounding voice as he discussed his plans with Wen. The Penetrator moved closer to be sure he missed nothing. Two major questions remained unanswered. How, from Wisconsin, did Thornesby intend to spread a flu epidemic across the country? And what sort of ultimatum was going to be made?

"How marvelously convenient a scapegoat the far-right political faction is. 'Militarists, super-patriots, the military-industrial complex, the Establishment,' all the catchphrases and epithets devised by the Marxists over the past few years to slander them, we can now use to mask our real intentions." He sobered suddenly. "But I'm wandering."

Further comment was cut off as Hal approached. He indicated the work in progress with a gesture. "Nearly finished, Doc. You want to run a test on everything before we start the launch?"

"We've missed the optimum time for this night, I'm afraid. With that storm front moving in, they'd never carry to the target area before daylight. Make sure everything is working right and, if the winds change and the front passes through today, make the launch about midnight."

After Hal returned to his work, Theo Wen took up their previous conversation. "I still don't understand how you can update Phase Two so easily."

"I'm leaving for California today. There's an early morning flight to Chicago from Green Bay. I can make connections there on TWA for Los Angeles. I'll be on the island by nightfall. Once the crew is assembled out there, we can start launching at any time."

California. Of course, the jet stream. The Penetrator had the answer to how Thornesby planned to spread disease across the country. At altitudes above thirty-thousand feet, strong, nearly constant winds—the jet stream—blew from west to east at high velocity. But that high up the temperature was extremely cold, in the $-10°$ to $-40°$ F range. How could the disease-causing organisms survive? The Penetrator stopped his speculation as Thornesby continued.

"Don't worry, there are enough insulated containers on hand to cover this part of the plan. By next week another 250 will be delivered," he said in answer to Wen's question, then added, "Even if we have to initiate Phase Three, we'll be ready."

Wen suppressed a shudder, his ill ease clear in the tone of his voice. "That's nasty stuff to deal with. Once started, could we really be sure of stopping it?"

Thornesby appeared not to have the slightest worry. "Of course. The army would ship antitoxin to the target areas, inoculate those not infected. They'd do our work for us. Now *there's* one those army idiots would approve of. Rocky Mountain Spotted Fever, plague—oh, a dozen others, dispensed by airplane from aerosol containers at high altitude. That's their way of doing it. In their plans for years. But when something innovative, really original comes up, they get all conscience stricken and say it is too inhumane. They'll comply with our demands, or we'll give them a dose of their own medicine, by God."

"And—and Phase Three will be conducted from out there?" Wen asked, trying to get the slightly mad Thornesby back on the track.

"There—and here in part. The main objective will be the East Coast: New York, Washington, Boston. The bureaucrats don't give a damn what happens west of the Blue Ridge Mountains. Why should they? Their jobs are secure. No, the way to make them hurt, to pay attention, is to scare *them*, make *them* sick, strike at *their* families. And the politicians? There will be demands for them to do something, anything, to stop it. They'll comply all right; they will have no choice."

"There is such a thing as going too far."

"Theo—Theo, I know that. Rest assured I won't activate Phase Three without coordination and approval from you and your people—or as a last resort."

The Penetrator had to act. He must destroy this place before another launch of the deadly bacteria could be completed. Yet there was this unknown island base. Where was it, and what did Thornesby intend to release from there besides the flu virus? It must be located and wiped out too. His only lead to the place was the insane bacteriologist, Creighton Thornesby. Mark could short-circuit the scheme by killing the mad doctor, he realized.

But the *potential* for disaster would remain. What proof he had was surmise and personally obtained evidence which, considering the source, he could never turn over to the authorities and expect them to act against a fellow bureaucrat. No, Creighton Thornesby would have to be spared for the time being. But this place had to go.

"Hadn't you better go?" Wen asked. "It's past two a.m. now, and it's a long drive to Green Bay."

"Yes, yes. I'll be on my way. Well, onward and . . . upward." Creighton Thornesby's parting laughter was high pitched, a little wild, ragged around the edges.

Chapter 12

TRAVELING DOOM

Creighton Thornesby was paged for a long-distance call by the Northcentral Airlines ticket desk at Green Bay's Austin Straubel Air Field. He responded only to receive grim news.

"He hit us again. The Penetrator."

"What do you mean, Theo?" Thornesby demanded.

"Somehow he located the new place, burned it like the first one. Garotted one guard and used some sort of fire bomb. We managed to save only a few crates and the gas generator."

"Damn! You say he killed only one man? If the Penetrator is as tough as you said, why didn't he finish all of you?"

Theophilus Wen felt genuine fear. Gone was his supercilious, precise manner of speech. "I don't know. It all happened so fast. Everything was quiet, then the sound of glass breaking and flames everywhere. We got out all we could.

117

Hal's going to have to cook up a new batch, so no more launches for a while."

"I—I can't come back now. This is even more reason for going all out on Phase Two. I'm going on the California. Have Hal use the *my caline cytose* culture. He'll find it in the refrigerator at the office in Wausau. It grows fastest and is most prolific. And—find a new, secure place, understand? Also make sure everyone takes his final flu vaccine shot. You and I have ours, but we have to protect the men."

Before Thornesby had left the farm the previous night, the Penetrator had disengaged himself from his listening post, slipped back to his car and eased down to a culvert that granted access to a field, coasting in behind a hedgerow. Then he made another rapid inventory of his chances. He knew where Thornesby was going, at least the first two legs to L.A., and the Mooney at 195 mph would beat a car to Green Bay from Wausau. That left time to eliminate the germ factory. How?

If only he had a weapon. Anything would do. He had matches, though. Perhaps he could burn them out again. Though how could he reach the inside through a crew that was charged up, edgy after the previous incident and the move? He needed a rapid means of getting a blaze going.

Moonlight glinted off shiny metal and glass in the ditch, evidence of civilization's encroachment of these rural environs. For once, Mark was glad for the presence of man's most common spoor—litter. When Thornesby roared past, on his way to Wausau, the Penetrator hurried to the shallow drainage trench and retrieved several empty beer bottles. If only he had a piece of hose—a Watts credit card—he could siphon out enough gasoline to make a dozen molotov cocktails. That was, of course, doing it the hard way.

Crawling under the rear of the Granada, the Penetrator clenched his penlight in his teeth while he used the buckle of his Protecto-Belt as a makeshift wrench to loosen the drain valve. He was rewarded with a pungent tingle of gasoline. He held one bottle after another under the slim flow until he had six full ones. Then he shut off the gas, gathered his volatile cargo, and set off for the farm.

Normal routine had been restored, Mark discovered, when he was fifty yards from the barn. Too normal for their own good. Only a single exterior guard, Randy, had been posted. The Penetrator hadn't the time to make a study of Randy's patrol route and timing. He had to set his fires and get after Creighton Thornesby. He nestled his gasoline bombs among clumps of fresh-sprouting alfalfa and removed the piano wire garotte from his belt pouch. Quietly he slipped up on the sentry.

The thin wire loop flashed in the moonlight as the Penetrator whipped it over the unsuspecting Randy's head. Snapping his crossed wrists back to normal position as the wire bit deeply into soft flesh, the Penetrator kinked it tightly so that holding would not be necessary. Then he lifted the struggling man off his feet and held him until death provided ultimate relaxation. Mark eased Randy to the ground, retrieved his scratch-made incendiary bombs, and closed in on the barn.

He sat one, unlighted, at the large doors in the rear, rounded the building and placed a second at a side door. Lighting the third, he hurled it onto the roof. Numbers four and five smashed into blazing fury against the sides of the barn, the sixth down the narrow front. He ran quickly to the first two and lit their wicks. The Penetrator paused only a second to insure a good blaze, then trotted to his car. He had to catch a plane.

Once in the air, heading southeast toward Green Bay, the Penetrator made a change in plans. He would fly directly to O'Hare and pick up Thornesby in the TWA boarding area. In the larger airport, there was less chance of the criminal doctor recognizing Mark, and it was necessary to be aboard the same flight. He programmed the flight director and auto-pilot for O'Hare in Chicago and leaned back to rest, letting the airplane fly itself. Then he reached for the telephone.

A relatively new convenience accessory for general aviation, the radio telephone unit, a King KT96, twelve-channel rig, provided Mark quick contact with the Stronghold. Once Professor Haskins answered, Mark attached his portable scrambler and briefed his staff on what had happened so far. Next Mark asked a question that had bothered him since hearing Thornesby's announcement of his trip to California. Where, off the West Coast, could there be an island suitable to launching disease-filled balloons? Quiz the computer, he instructed. He also asked that the 1957 Chevy be brought to LAX, the international terminal, the key left at the TWA passenger service desk.

The Penetrator would need it to tail Thornesby when the doctor left the airport. A '57 model Chevrolet was not an uncommon sight on Southern California streets—even Mark's, in mint, if dusty, condition. Hardly an eye-catcher for other than car buffs. Its outward appearance, though, never gave a hint of what waited within. The nearly four-hundred ponies of the Chrysler Hemi were fed through the Edelbrock manifold by four two-barrel carbs, blasting their power into a four-speed racing box, drive-trained to a 2:1 racing rear end. Mark had bought the road bomb, already built up, from a kid in San Bernardino. After removing the shackles and risers, he had been hard put to restore its outward appearance to stock with a factory-like paint job and hard-to-find original chrome. With its nearly constant and generous coating of desert dust, it looked like any one of thousands of four-wheeled denizens of east L.A. The hidden truth remained that it could keep up with or pass nearly anything on the road. The professor assured Mark that his car

121

would be waiting as near as possible to the TWA terminal, with a load of the Penetrator's "special" tools in the trunk. Professor Haskins said he would contact Mark later with the computer data. Mark broke the connection and leaned back to enjoy the ride.

Checking the chart and the back course to the Green Bay VORTAC, Mark cranked a slight correction in the heading, reaching for O'Hare. The auto-pilot examined the new data, checked it against information provided by the localizer and the outboard track from GBR VORTAC, then made a decision. The Mooney gracefully banked left and leveled out on the new heading.

The Guadalupes and the Coronados were off Mexico. They were desolate and sparsely settled, with little or no fresh water, but closely patrolled by Mexican authorities. There was even a police shack on Big Coronado. The Santa Barbaras, including Goat Island—Catalina—were out: hardly an acre that wasn't spilling over with the rich and near-rich, or fishermen and those engaged in the tourist trade. Nothing after that until Anacordas Island and further north the Queen Charlottes off British Columbia. Not much to choose from. Given an option play like that, the Penetrator thought, he'd settle for the Coronados. Risky, but barely possible.

Mark landed and arranged for tie-down at a small flight service operator near the Air Force

Reserve and Air National Guard airplane park. After completing his business, he headed to the main terminal at O'Hare.

There he was happy to discover that the Northcentral Airlines and TWA bays were next to each other with only a short walk between. In a convenience shop next to the Old English Pub, Mark puchased a short-crown, narrow-brim casual hat and matching windbreaker in light blue denim with thin red stripes, and a pair of wraparound sunglasses. It was a makeshift disguise, but by walking round-shouldered and maintaining a low profile, the Penetrator was confident of escaping Creighton Thornesby's notice.

Thornesby arrived fifteen minutes later and headed directly to the check-in counter at TWA Gate 4. Mark noted the flight number and hurried to the ticket desk. He purchased a one-way first-class ticket. Thornesby was in tourist, Mark had confirmed. He made it back to Gate 4 in ample time.

All seats on this flight were reserved, so the plane was loaded in reverse order, those in the smoking section bording first, then the non-smokers, and lastly first-class passengers. Thornesby had no opportunity to closely scrutinize Mark. Once the 727 was free of the boarding tunnel, Mark sat back and relaxed in the oversized, comfortable seat, playing at second-guessing the pilot—estimating run-up, rotation speed, wheels up, flaps retracted, and climb-out. He had nothing better to do until they reached Los Angeles four-and-a-half hours later.

Creighton Thornesby never left the terminal at L.A. International. With his single piece of carry-on luggage, he walked briskly from satellite to satellite until he stopped in front of the PSA counter. He purchased a one-way ticket to San Diego and headed for the boarding area.

Seated among the bustle of transients—families and well-wishers gathered to meet arrivals or send off departees—the Penetrator was an anonymous face in the crowd. He watched as Thornesby cleared through the gate, waited some ten minutes until the boarding announcement, then joined a line of others who were being swallowed by the open maw of the DC-9. Once the silver bird lumbered toward the taxi strip with Thornesby aboard, the Penetrator hurriedly left the terminal.

San Diego. It could only mean that Thornesby was headed to the islands off Mexico. There was only one other alternative, a small lump of land in the ocean, some ten miles to sea and seven miles south of San Diego. But it was, to Mark's recollection, even less promising than the Guadalupes or Coronados. Mark discounted the possibility that the demented scientist might be devious enough to use the flight to San Diego as a ruse, to double back and go elsewhere. What would be the reason?

For all Thornesby knew, his only threat, the Penetrator, was rampaging through Wisconsin after the doctor's underlings. No, barren and inhospitable as they may be, the islands off San Diego were Thornesby's destination. Gunning the big motor hidden under the modest hood of the '57 Chevy, the Penetrator left the airport, headed for the interchange to the San Bernardino freeway.

In an hour-and-a-half, he'd be at the Stronghold. The only way to stop Thornesby required the ability to make a quick reconnaissance and immediate strike. With a dozen islands to search, he counted on the Helio-Courier to provide that capability.

Chapter 13

MODIFIED ANSWER

"It is absolutely vital that we make the first launch tonight," Dr. Creighton Thornesby demanded of his head lab technician. They stood in front of a ground-colored, irregularly shaped laboratory building on Isla Perdida. The tiny dot of land in the Pacific was well named: Lost Island. On even the best of navigational charts, it showed no larger than a fly speck.

Only a few wind-twisted trees, ten to twenty feet tall at most, stood in widely separated, disheartened clumps. The ground sloped sharply up from tiny strips of beach, trying to be a mountain or high hill but, failing miserably, so folded in on itself that it resembled the convolutions of the human brain. Save the trees, enormous flocks of sea birds, and a few turtles, Isla Perdida presented a fruitless, forbidding face to those who ventured near.

Unseen by the few who risked strong currents and hidden rocks to come in close to Isla Perdida was the building where Creighton Thornesby set up his California death factory. Built into one of the deep arroyos, masked completely from observation seaward, it was constructed of native adobe, with not a single regular line or corner. Seven men had gathered on the island at Thornesby's request. The foreman stood stunned at their leader's orders.

"It's not possible. We only just managed to off-load the water, food, and other supplies we need before the boat had to get out of here because of the tide. The cultures we brought along are in stasis. They'll have to be restarted carefully. I would say late tomorrow afternoon will be the earliest."

"Why weren't the men kept here on a permanent basis? You knew the cultures they could have maintained would be needed on a moment's notice."

"First, there's the supply problem. The generators needed to operate the lab would have gobbled up more gas per day than the men used water or food. Secondly, even if we had undertaken to provide necessary materials, there was the risk of discovery. Right now Isla Perdida is a sort of no-man's land. Neither the U.S. nor Mexico wants to claim it, too far out at sea. Only the best navigational charts even bother to name it; the others merely indicate the presence of rocks and shoals. But if word got back from fishing boats and yachtsmen that someone was prowling around out here, the situation would change rapidly enough. We'd have a Mexican gunboat and a Coast Guard cutter standing offshore in a matter of hours. Two-hundred-mile limit or not, the Mexicans would be wrangling with our government from now to doomsday over who had a right to this place. If you wanted to keep this operation secret, we couldn't afford the risk."

Mollified, Thornesby altered his plans. "Tomorrow afternoon. I'm not in favor of a daylight launch. We'll reschedule for an hour after full darkness tomorrow night."

"Low-level winds at that time are offshore. The best time to avoid detection would be to launch into the setting sun."

"We'll do it that way then." Thornesby started to the doorway of the lab. "Let's get those cultures to working before anything else is done."

Mark instinctively ducked his head, although there was no need to, as he walked out from under the leading edge of the Helio-Courier's left wing. Here, in the underground hangar at the Stronghold, the Penetrator gradually made progress toward converting his high-wing bird into a combat aircraft.

"That's the last of the brackets," he told David Red Eagle. "We can start on the wiring. With any luck we'll be testing the circuits in an hour."

Red Eagle's craggy, seamed face remained impassive, although a gleam of admiration and affection lit his eye. Mark was as close to him as any of the nine sons he had sired. Closer, if truth were told. Over the incredible number of years since his birth, Red Eagle had observed the best and the worst among his people. The strength and quickness of his youth had left him, but in their place came wisdom. It was his conviction, based on knowledge and experience, that this half-Welsh, half-Cheyenne young man, Mark Hardin, was by far the greatest of all of them.

David Red Eagle, like Mark, had attended college, but he had gone during that time when few Native American children completed six years of grammar school, let alone became students in a university. His education, though, had only begun when he left the halls of formal academia. Schooled by the old men—the singers, storytellers, and medicine men of many tribes—in the Powers and the ways of nature, Red Eagle had imparted this wealth of knowledge to Mark.

Armed with the Strong Heart of *Sho-tu-ça* and the martial arts prowess of *Orenda Keowa*, Mark—on his forays as the Penetrator—was truly formidable. But Red Eagle had not let it rest on the ways of the past. He had carefully and thoroughly steeped himself and his pupil in the latest technology of the twentieth century. These odd-looking modifications to the Helio-Courier were only the latest extension of that learning experience.

"You'll have to fly low to avoid detection on radar," Red Eagle said, as Mark began attaching the first of two unorthodox wiring harnesses. "How are you going to avoid having someone spot the changes you are making?"

"I've given that a lot of thought and—I'm still in the dark. If I had time enough, I could build a lightweight frame of wood, cover it with fabric, and dope it. Make a pod, in other words. But the drying and reapplications would take days."

"It is said that if one wants to hide something, it is best to conceal it in plain sight."

Mark looked blankly back at his mentor, as fully award of the first dictum of espionage as the old Indian. Then his face suddenly lit up with excitement. "Of course. That's it. If I can't hide them, make them appear to be something they aren't. I can attach long, colored streamers to the rear of each tube, make them look like smoke generators for an airshow. From more than three-hundred feet away, those fiberglass cylinders can't be recognized for what they are anyway."

Aided by Red Eagle, Mark quickly went back to work, and they soon were able to test the firing circuits, making sure they would work as expected when needed. Then, in each set of brackets, the Penetrator placed the fiberglass tube of a disposable LAW antitank rocket. With slight modification each mechanism was attached to bare ends of wire so that it would fire from inside the cabin. Mark made a final check, topped off the fuel tanks, and wiped his hands on a shop cloth.

"Let's wheel her out. Time for a close look at the offshore islands."

At a cruising speed of well over 150 mph, the Penetrator made the 230 air miles from the Calico Mountains to the Coronado Islands in a little more than two hours' time. Keeping low, acting like a typical part of the general aviation traffic that abounded from the hundreds of pea-patch airports in Southern California, the Penetrator was able to avoid special attention. He began a gradual climb as Point Loma fell off behind him, coming in over the islands at six-thousand feet.

He made his first pass heading south over the three islands, aiming for the Guadalupes to eliminate them as suspect. He held off his descent until he was well past the small group, far to the west and south. An hour later he knew that the southernmost islands were clean. Drifting north, coming back with the sun at his tail, Mark made a close scrutiny of each island of the Coronado chain. Twice around each was all it took. By process of elimination, that left Isla Perdida. The tiny scrap of land lay somewhat north and west of his present position. Mark pointed the Helio-Courier in the proper direction, wondering again if Thornesby had managed to throw him off by a trip to San Diego while the real destination lay elsewhere.

It took three passes around Isla Perdida to locate the camouflaged laboratory. As he turned to make a verification run, figures emerged from the building, two of them struggling against the wind with a partially inflated weather balloon.

As Mark lined up the spinner to make his first attack, the men gestured upward at the Helio-Courier, heads bobbing in excited conversation. They released the balloon, which leaped skyward as the Penetrator flipped switches, firing the outboard two rockets.

The left-hand rocket missed entirely, striking the steep arroyo wall behind the laboratory. Right on its tail, the second missile blasted into the roof of the building. Gouts of dust and debris erupted into the air, obscuring the target. Mark turned away to line up again as the men rushed inside. He completed a three-sixty while more workers, burdened by their gas bag armful, hurried outside. Five more balloons wobbled into the air before Mark was in the slot. As quickly as they let go, Thornesby's cohorts dashed back for more. Inexorably the Helio-Curier bore down on them.

It seemed like hours as the seconds passed until he came in range, then Mark flipped two more switches and a pair of Light Antitank Weapon rockets roared toward the target. Direct hits blasted thick chunks of adobe from the front wall, covering the area with more dust. Mark banked left this time, giving the high-winged bird full throttle. As the target dwindled at the far end of his turn, he noticed he was taking ground fire.

Time to worry about that later. He had two more rockets to loose. They would, he hoped,

133

demolish Thornesby's citadel of death. Easing the plane into a shallow dive, Mark reached for the switches, holding fire until the spinner centered on the open doorway of the lab. With a flick of his forefinger, the Penetrator sent high explosive death sizzling toward Creighton Thornesby on tails of smoke and flame. He delayed his turnout until he saw the missiles strike at both sides of the door, blasting a larger hole in the crumbling corner of the tortured structure.

Hauling back on the control, the Penetrator noticed an increase in ground fire as he sped after the climbing balloons. A rare form of virus that caused a violent and debilitating influenza, Mark had heard Thornesby tell his partner in crime. Mark knew he would have to stop the silent carriers of this epidemic before he could finish with those on the island. Closing in on the first balloon, he opened the side window, reaching for his Mossberg M500 ATP that lay on the right-hand seat.

He poked the muzzle of the shotgun outside as the first grayish-purple envelope loomed large ahead of him. A light kick of rudder peddle, and he squeezed off a round. A three-inch Magnum load of Number 6 shot demolished the five-foot-diameter balloon but triggered the break-open mechanism of the small black box that hung below the nozzle. It filled the air with flat pieces of plastic, styrofoam insulation, and highly virulent viruses.

The Penetrator wasn't worried as the prop-blast threw the contaminated air into the cabin. In Mark's condition, with proper treatment, there seemed little chance to him of being killed by the germs, no matter how much exposure. He could always take care of his own decontamination after the job was done. Now he was busy lining up on a second bearer of ill wind. Another slight maneuver and sharp report from the Mossberg, and the silent disease carrier ceased to be. Mark swung wide to avoid the area and closed with yet another.

Seven rounds of three-inch Magnum 12-gauge loads demolished seven balloons, but the Penetrator had run out of ammunition in the magazine. As he turned to line up on another target, he stuffed shells into the underside tube. His mode of attack was taking too long, he realized, as he completed a one-eighty. As he had maneuvered to blast individual targets, the men on the ground were releasing a constant stream of deadly floating bombs. A new tactic was required.

Diving into a rising, arching line of balloons, the Penetrator destroyed them with wing tips and propeller blades. The result splashed his airplane and himself with flu virus. In the distance between the first and second balloons, Mark contemplated his situation. Even in this day of miracle drugs, there were always a few who died from influenza. Would a microscopic crystal accomplish what bullets had so far failed to do? But Mark dismissed the worrisome thoughts as the second target splashed open on the leading edge of his left wing. All he needed to do was polish off Thornesby's launch site and fly back to the Stronghold. Once on the ground, the virus could be identified, isolated, and defeated. The powers of *Sho-tu-ça* and those of modern medicine, if necessary, made the risk safe enough to hazard. At least it seemed a good idea when the Penetrator first reasoned it out.

Then he began to take heavier ground fire. A line of holes appeared along the cowling. A sudden spray of oil spattered the windshield, black smoke belched from the exhaust, and the manifold pressure dropped rapidly. The oil temperature gauge indicated far over to the right of the red line. The Helio-Courier gave a coughing lurch, and the engine died. Mark was flying a dead airplane.

With the power off, struggling with the sluggish controls, the Penetrator set the Helio-Courier into a slow spiral, seeking a place to let down. As he did, his mind replayed his earlier thought, this time to a different tune. Stranded on this island, how soon could he expect to reach a competent doctor? Could the virus be identified? Did treatment even exist?

Sweat broke out on Mark's brow, and his palms felt slick and clammy as he urged his wounded craft toward some sort of safety. How soon would symptoms occur? Where could he land? What chance did he have?

Chapter 14

CRACK UP

Pulling up tight on his racing thoughts, the Penetrator took a careful look at the terrain as he came in low over Isla Perdida.

His glance revealed no level ground where a dead-stick landing could be made. Updrafts buffeted the gliding airplane, and it took all Mark's ability and concentration to keep in level flight as he sought some alternative. There was the beach, a dangerously soft, narrow band all around the island, and there were several stands of small, twisted trees. His choices seemed to be slim and none.

If the Helio-Courier nosed over on, or just after, touchdown on the beach, with Thornesby's men still on the island, he'd not live long enough to know what germ had infected him. At best he'd be banged up a little and left with a battle on his hands. The alternative was too impossible to consider.

Although he had read about such a landing several years ago in an issue of *Flying* magazine, and even though the manufacturer had made mention of it being possible in an early sales brochure, Mark had little faith in the idea of landing in a tree! Setting down like a bird on a calm day seemed too much to ask. Reason was against it. Yet, there was more than one claim that it could be done. The nearer to the ground he came, the sharper his rate of descent increased. The time for decisions had come.

Easing back on the stick, Mark gave a mental shrug and headed toward a stand of low, sinuous evergreens that lay directly ahead of him on the hilly horizon. Hoping for the hopeless to be true, he began setting up for a rough landing.

Using the manual trim and rudder pedals, he positioned the Helio-Courier in an approach to the trees. With a loud pop the automatic wing slots along the leading edge of both wings flew open, slowing his air speed even more. The battery provided barely strength enough to extend the flaps. There would be time enough for only one try. If he failed, he would crash and burn. Cautiously he lost altitude a few feet at a time. Then the trees were dead ahead, growing rapidly despite his decreasing airspeed. All switches off. Mark jerked his shoulder harness tightly against him, flicked his eyes to check seat belt and strap connections. Then, as the first green branches disappeared under the leading edge of the wings, he hauled violently back on the stick. The airspeed indicator nosedived to 40 mph.

The Helio-Courier nosed up into a sudden stall, dropping tail first into the trees. There followed a fierce rending of metal, splintering of branches, and singing crack of breaking plexiglas as the big craft settled earthward. The steel cage cabin construction buckled and groaned in protest while the wings flopped up and down as if a prehistoric proto-bird were seeking to take flight.

Jagged branches pierced the floor and surged upward until the Helio-Courier came to rest suddenly. The violent action of seconds before subsided to a gentle rocking, the wings sagging, their tips still oscillating gradually. The special roll-bar type steel cage of the Helio's cabin had saved the Penetrator from grisly death, impaled on a shaft of shattered wood. Mark's chest ached as if every rib had been broken in three places, his bladder felt as though it had burst, and he bled from a slight cut on his forehead. But he was down and the Penetrator felt fine . . . just great!

Mark unfastened the restraining straps and gathered up his shotgun and a bag of ammunition for it, along with his .45. He lowered them to the ground at the end of a nylon cord. Then he climbed from the airplane and painfully worked his way down.

Mark's spectacular landing had been witnessed by Thornesby and his men. Three of them toiled breathlessly up the steep slope to the small ridge where the Helio-Courier rested in the trees. As they neared, one spotted Mark moving and threw a rifle to his shoulder. The round was triggered off into the air, though, as a charge of No. 4 buckshot smashed into his chest. The others scattered and began returning the Penetrator's fire.

Mark edged through the sparse concealment of the trees and scant cover of rocky outcrops, maneuvering to get a shot at the other men. Below him he saw six more balloons being released. Then more of Creighton Thornesby's troops headed toward the slope, weapons at the ready.

As reinforcements arrived, two men charged the Penetrator's last position, running close together in the worst example of combat efficiency Mark had seen in years. He reached into the tough olive drab musette bag and extracted a five-round cardboard box. He inserted two into the magazine tube and cycled the action. The new 12-gauge fodder had converted his shotgun into a grenade launcher. Printed in black on the OD-colored box was the legend: "PROJECTILE, M-34 (Restricted)." The charge burst just in front of the rushing gunmen, spraying them with thin slivers of sharpened surgical steel.

Blood flew from their faces, necks, and chests as they tumbled face forward into the dirt. Another man stood, firing off a stubby-barreled submachine gun. The second round detonated beside his head, turning it into a fine red mist as the slicing metal strips shredded him to pulp above the ear lobes. The remaining troops broke, withdrawing downhill toward the laboratory.

Mark was behind them, firing with unremitting precision, unconcerned with the screaming ricochets of unaimed, hurried shots thrown in his general direction. Far below on the beach, the muffled sound of a power boat rose, causing Mark to stop, listening. Then he saw motion as a red and white Chris Craft broke from the shelter of overhanging rocks and sped out into the sea. The Penetrator easily recognized the familiar profile of Creighton Thornesby at the wheel.

Panic seemed to seize the ditched crew when their leader deserted them. They barricaded themselves inside the lab and fired at the slightest sound or movement. Carefully the Penetrator worked himself down to the building, standing at last on the roof near a hole blasted by his rockets.

"Put up your hands and come out. You won't be hurt. Thornesby's deserted you. You have no other choice. Now move!"

Zinging torrents of lead, from a variety of weapons, answered the Penetrator's demand. When the firing subsided, he tried again.

"This is your last chance. Come out and you won't be harmed in any way. It's Creighton Thornesby I'm after. Surrender and you'll be left here for the authorities. There won't even be a mention of automatic weapons. Besides, you're exposed to the flu virus; you need medical aid."

Another fusillade buzzed and sang through the opening in the roof, forcing Mark to retreat for

141

a moment. As the last shot blasted away, an answering voice called defiantly to the Penetrator.

"The Feds find out what we were up to and it'll be our ass. We're vaccinated against the virus. It's your butt that's in a sling. You gotta come in and get us."

Reluctantly the Penetrator reached into his musette bag. His hand closed on the smooth, round casing of an M-27 fragmentation grenade. Having triple the fifty-percent kill radius of an old-fashioned M-3 fragger, it would turn the inside of the laboratory into a charnel house. Mark edged to the rim of the jagged hole, left index finger hooked in the safety pin ring.

"No more talk, fella. Come on out or I'll blow you out with a grenade."

"Fuck you!" the defiant one shouted. More slugs thudded into the adobe roof or shrilled their way through empty air.

The Penetrator pulled the pin, slipped the spoon, and counted a quick two. Then he dropped the hand bomb over the edge. The sharp *crang* of the exploding grenade was deadened somewhat by the thick adobe structure, then replaced by the screams of the dying. As the furor died down inside, the Penetrator worked his way off the roof and around to the blasted-out doorway.

Mark examined the dead inside and the debris of Thornesby's venture. He felt sick at heart at these needless deaths. If only they had surrendered. These men would have faced no more than a few years in prison. Sighing, the Penetrator shook his black mood. Then he dragged the bodies outside, returned to gather up a pile of combustible material, and set fire to the building. Out in the tangy sea air, Mark paused to make sure the interior burned lustily, then started uphill to his crashed airplane.

Up in the tree, fifteen feet above the ground, Mark opened both drain valves on the fuel tanks and crawled down quickly. The Helio-Courier had served him faithfully and well. He hated to do what he knew he must. Although the registry number and engine number were not those with which the bird began life, he had to make sure there was no way of tracing it back to him, even under a cover name. To do that he had to destroy the evidence. This gallant lass of the air had saved his life, and he felt a lump in his throat as he searched a pocket for matches. As he struck a flame from the matchbook, the Penetrator suddenly realized he regretted this more than taking the lives of Thornesby's henchmen. The Helio-Courier, at least, hadn't been shooting back at him.

As the pool of gasoline blazed to fury, Mark turned away and trotted, shoulders sagging, toward the beach.

Within fifteen minutes of the Helio-Courier's explosion, which sent a billowing cloud of black smoke high into the air, nearly a dozen vessels circled off Isla Perdida. Sail craft and power boats alike worked in as close as possible. Aboard

143

the most daring one, two people spotted the lone figure standing on the beach. They waved and called, working their way cautiously closer. The tall, dark man gave only brief acknowledgement of their presence.

When the boat was as close as it could safely approach the island, two broad-shouldered men lowered a small dinghy, fired up the three-horse motor, and one of them piloted it in to the beach. He climbed, sun bronzed and smiling, over the gunwale and called greetings to Mark.

"What happened, mister? Why the fires?"

"I . . . ah, I crashed here on the island. My plane burned."

"You get off a message before you hit?"

"No I didn't," the Penetrator replied.

"Well, then, better hop aboard. We'll take you in to San Diego."

Mark thought of his contamination by the flu virus and raised a warning hand. "No. I . . . that is, shouldn't I wait for the Coast Guard or something?"

"Never mind. We have a radio aboard the *Tradewinds*. We can let them know and get you in a lot sooner than they can. Besides, then you can make your explanations with a stiff drink in your hand and another under your belt."

"All right," Mark relented. Despite the danger he represented to the others until he had been decontaminated, his need to go after Creighton Thornesby loomed greater. He waded into the shallow surf and climbed into the skiff. In minutes they were back at the large motor-sailer, being hoisted aboard.

The *Tradewinds* made the long reach to San Diego Bay easily, although darkness had overtaken them before the boat tacked out of sight of Isla Perdida. Mark had made desultory small talk with the curious and excited people aboard—two couples from Newport—and accepted a strong drink. Later, he had eaten his fill of small bonita delicately fried in olive oil, and hash browns, with his rescuers and topped it off with an icy Bohemia ale. As they raised the Point Loma light, Mark went out on deck with one of the men.

"Look, there's more to it than I told you earlier. I didn't want to worry the girls. There's some sort of strange contamination on that island. It did in some men who were camping there, and I must have caught it after I crashed."

"What do you mean, contamination?"

"It's a virus infection, actually. When you get in, tell the Coast Guard. They'll take you to the Public Health people and get it taken care of. Chances are all four of you have been exposed by picking me up."

"When *we* get in? What about you?"

"I . . . ah, for reasons of my own, I don't want to spend hours talking with the Coast Guard."

The Penetrator's rescuer grew cold, slightly withdrawn. "I don't like the sound of that."

"I didn't ask you to. I appreciate what you've

145

done. But there's a point beyond which you have no need to know. There's no way I can properly thank you for getting me off that island, and now I think I may be the cause of all of you getting very sick. All the same, for your protection report your suspected infection to U.S. Public Health Service. And . . . " the Penetrator paused, fishing in one jacket pocket for a small paper-wrapped package. He handed it to his host. "Here, Jack. Open this after I've gone."

Before Jack could protest, the Penetrator slipped over the side and swam with strong strokes toward the lights of Harbor Island. Slowly Jack opened the parcel he held in one hand.

"Him!" he exclaimed when he saw what was inside. "I'll be damned. Right on my boat. I will be double damned." He swung the wheel, directing his boat toward the Coast Guard station. As he lined up on the dock lights, he slipped the blue flint arrowhead into his pocket, determined to forget all about it while in the presence of officialdom.

Chapter 15

PLAGUE FARM

The Penetrator had a fair idea where Creighton Thornesby would head after making his escape from Isla Perdida. Yet the Penetrator's task had now reached monumental proportions. How could he stop the berserk scientist before Thornesby initiated another part of his diabolical scheme? Answer: he had to get to Wisconsin fast.

But because of his contamination by the virulent and prolific flu bug, Mark ruled out commercial jet travel. What he needed was a rental biz jet, though that was out of the question. He hadn't time to get checked out in one. The problem of transportation would have to wait. Other things claimed first priority.

Mark's impromptu swim in the bay had not sufficed to properly decontaminate him. He shivered as he waited in the darkness on the beach for his clothes to dry. Then he walked to the nearest pharmacy and purchased a bottle of the strongest antiseptic soap available without a prescription. Leaving the drugstore, the Penetrator started the long walk over the hump of Loma Portal to Ocean Beach. A little less than two hours later, he reached his destination and took a room at a no-questions-asked, $3.50 a night hotel. Once in his room, he stripped and showered thoroughly in the hottest water his body could stand. His clothes received the same treatment and, clad in a large towel wrapped around his middle, Mark went to the pay phone in the hall.

The Penetrator's first call was to the Stronghold. He asked for a pilot's license, a log book with matching name and appropriate hours entered, fresh clothes, and some light armament. Then he explained what had happened.

"It looks like I blew it. With the main man still on the loose, I have to get back there," Mark concluded. "Have Red Eagle get on the road with those things. Also, I need the location of any other farms owned by Wen and his cabal."

"Easy enough. There are seven others we know of. Although that's not to say there might be more." Professor Haskins gave Mark the directions to find the farms. "I have an alternative plan, though, my boy. It's a four-hour drive down there from here. Why don't I have David take me over to Riverside? I can charter a plane and be at Lindberg Field in a little over an hour-and-a-half."

Mark appreciated the supreme effort this maneuver took. Normally reticent to leave the

Stronghold for a visit to the marginally metropolitan area of Barstow, Professor Haskins had taken the emergency in stride and now stood ready to hazard exposure to the "civilization" from which he had withdrawn ten years before. A functional team depended upon the ability of all its members to grasp any situation and act accordingly regardless of circumstances. The logistics of maintaining a combat force in the field—be it a division or a single man—demanded it. The Penetrator felt blessed with the best team ever activated. His admiration at the professor's sacrifice colored the tone of his voice.

"All right, we'll work it that way. And . . . thanks."

Mark's next call was for airline passenger service.

"I'm sorry, sir. There are no direct flights out of San Diego to Chicago or the northcentral states tonight. The first one would be at seven-thirty tomorrow morning, with a stopover in Denver."

"What about connections through Los Angeles?"

"One moment, sir." After a pause, the pleasant-voiced young woman came back on the line. "You could leave here on Pacific Southwest Airlines at ten-forty, arriving LAX at eleven p.m., with connections by TWA to Chicago at eleven-fifty, making stops in Denver and Wichita. There are no connections from Chicago to Green

149

Bay or Iron Mountain until six-thirty a.m., by Northcentral Airlines."

"Was there any earlier flight that would have connected with Northcentral?"

"Yes, sir. One that left here at seven-twenty, with stops in Los Angeles and Denver. That would be TWA."

Thornesby could never have reached San Diego in time for that one. It looked as if Creighton Thornesby was as stranded in this city of ¾ million as he. It gave the Penetrator a slight edge, but how good a one? Mark dug into the yellow pages again.

He found what he wanted and dialed a number at Montgomery Field on Kearney Mesa. He got an answer on the third ring.

"Mustang Air Service."

After a few preliminaries, the Penetrator got to the main question. "You wouldn't happen to have a P-51 available, would you?"

"I do. Got two of them. But they aren't for rent."

"Look, I need a fast airplane for a cross-country trip. Something that'll cruise above three-hundred."

"Why don't you try Flying Tigers at Lindberg? They have a turbo-prop that'll cruise at three-twenty-five. You can charter or fly it yourself if you're checked out."

"Thanks. I'll give 'em a holler."

"Tell them Andy at Mustang sent you."

"You bet."

Fifteen minutes later Mark had arranged for a checkout in the Cessna 410 owned by Flying Tigers Airline. Mark returned to his room, mentally planning his trip. The seventeen-hundred air miles to Chicago could be covered with a single fuel stop at Denver. The flight would last between five-and-a-half to six hours, taking advantage of the pressurized cabin and the jet stream. Given the avionics aboard and the autopilot, Mark figured he could snooze part of the way. If he got out before midnight, he might make it to Wisconsin ahead of Thornesby.

He had to make it that way. Every precious minute counted heavily. With seven farms to investigate in order to locate the exact spot the mad doctor would scurry to, the Penetrator would have to change in Chicago to his Mooney and fly directly to the airport nearest to the cluster of dairies and move out from there. Thwarted at every point so far, Thornesby might go completely overboard. The Penetrator didn't want the public to learn the deadly meaning of Phase Three before he did.

Phase Three would be devastating. That much he had learned before his dash to the West Coast. Now Mark worked at fighting the effects of the flu mentally, feeling at a loss because of uncertainty over its nature. The mental effort restored at least part of his strength and cleared his mind of nonessentials. He was relaxed and ready, out the door at the first ring of the hall phone, an hour later.

"This is Flight Service at Lindberg Field. Is a Mr. Arrowsmith there?"

"This is he."

"We've been asked to contact you to let you know the charter flight you are expecting will be in about fifteen minutes from now."

"Do you still have contact with them?"

"We can get it."

"Would you ask the pilot to taxi to the Flying Tigers Airlines hangar?"

"Will do."

"Thanks."

Mark's check ride in the Cessna 410 was shorter than he had expected. Half an hour shooting instrument approaches to Lindberg Field, emergency procedures, and a high-altitude course out and back, parallel to the Laguna Mountains, got it signed off in his log. He agreed to an enormous rental fee, loaded his gear, and was ready to depart. His clothes had been damp but wearable when he left the hotel, but he gambled time over distance against the danger of exposing another innocent to the flu by taking a taxi. He arrived a few minutes ahead of the professor. He changed in the hangar restroom and, after brief farewells, boarded the twin-engine bird and fired up the whispering turbines.

After climb-out at his assigned departure altitude, Mark punched in altitude and heading, trimmed out for a smooth ascent to cruising altitude of 33,000, and catnapped while the auto-pilot flew him to Denver. He awakened in ample time to make an unhurried descent and landing.

The Denver papers were headlining the outbreak of a strange epidemic of a rare flu, highly virulent, with an incubation period of only a few hours. The contagion factor was astronomical, a Public Health Service officer was quoted as saying. Mark didn't need the newspaper story to advise him of the disease and its symptoms. His head throbbed, his nose ran, and a searing dryness made his throat a constant agony. While his plane was refueled, the Penetrator made a quick trip to the men's room, gulped three aspirins, and bought a large carton of coffee to go. Then he was off the ground again.

By the time Mark reached Chicago, his physical debility had succumbed to the remarkable powers of his mind. Through the healing arts of *Shotu-ça*, he had isolated the cause of his illness, compressed it, and cast it from him. That was not to say that the virus didn't remain in his system. It did—only now it had ceased to cause outward physical symptoms or to deplete his stamina. As he taxied away from the active runway, a dull headache still plagued him, but he felt restored and able to continue his quest.

Mark turned in the turbo-prop—Flying Tigers had a cross-rental agreement with an outfit at O'Hare. The hourly fee on the Hobbs Meter put a respectable dent in his cash reserve. Quickly he set out to cross the field to his Mooney. Warm-up

153

and takeoff instructions completed, Mark rammed N201PB into the air, northbound for his final encounter with Creighton Thornesby.

"I don't believe it. He was there, I tell you," Creighton Thornesby told Theophilus Wen as they walked to Wen's car in the parking lot at Green Bay's airport. "It had to be the Penetrator. One man and one airplane, and they destroyed our entire operation. It's as though he knew every move we planned to make before we did."

"Relax. You're safe enough now. We've relocated and, if it was he out in California, he has no way of knowing where we're at. Besides, use your head. He must have been exposed to the virus. If that's the case, he'll be flat on his back by now."

Thornesby thought that over a moment. "The way he dived on those balloons, he must have been saturated with the culture. The odds are he'll be dead by tonight." That lifted his spirits, and he walked with a more confident step, giving a short bark of laughter. "I like that. Yes, the Penetrator is as good as dead right now."

Mark Hardin landed at Mohawk Airport in Rhinelander, Wisconsin, well ahead of Thornesby's arrival in Green Bay. He obtained a rental car and off-loaded his arsenal, making sure the heavy weaponry was well represented. Armed with the locations of Wen's other farms, he drove

154

to the county courthouse and located them on the assessor's map.

After the third blank try, the Penetrator felt as though he were driving in circles toward a hopeless goal. The launch site could be located at any one of a dozen or more unknown places. Petty annoyances became major obstacles as he constantly struggled to stay ahead of the virus that raged through his body. He lacked sleep and proper nourishment and dipped deeply into his reserves to maintain coherent action. The breaking point was near; the limit beyond which his powers could no longer sustain him could come at any time. Yet the Penetrator's determination to stop Thornesby, to crush his mad scheme beyond any possibility of future use, continued to drag him onward. Driven by this compulsion, Mark checked his map and headed for the fourth dairy on the list.

It was late afternoon, the sun sliding low toward the western horizon, when the Penetrator made his first pass by the fifth farm. His brief, casual glance showed evidence of activity in the yard and around the barn. It wasn't, he noted, typically farm-related business. On his second run along the road, half an hour later, another car stood in the farmyard. It was a familiar vehicle, the one driven by Theophilus Wen. Mark drove to the mile corner, turned right, then right again a mile later, bringing himself up behind Thornesby's lair.

The Penetrator checked his weapons, selecting

what he would take on the assault. Satisfied, he slipped Ava, his plastic-bodied, CO_2-powered dart pistol, into the right-hand shoulder holster, the Star PD, short-barreled .45 auto into the left. He shrugged into a small shoulder pack that was loaded with ammunition and phosphorous grenades. Taking his Mossberg M500 ATP at high port, he moved off across a broad, rolling pasture, the setting sun at his back.

Inside the barn the National Weather Service advisory slowly droned out the temperatures, barometric pressures, winds, and precipitation conditions across the country. Creighton Thornesby spoke to himself as he caught the East Coast report.

"Good, it's raining in New York and Washington." To his workmen, he cautioned, "Altitude is entirely critical in this launch. We want those balloons to burst at about seven-thousand feet, so the rain will carry the plague bacillus down over a wide area."

"So this is Phase Three, bubonic plague," Wen said uncomfortably.

"Yes, the Black Plague of the Middle Ages. So appropriate, don't you think? We had some difficulty setting this one up. The problem was how to keep them below the altitude where they'd explode from internal pressure until the exact area was reached. Hal came up with the solution. A small bag of ballast suspended below the air bag, containing a timed, spring-loaded device to slit open the canvas and release the sand at the precise moment to allow the balloon to rise.

"These balloons are designed to destruct at a given difference between internal and external pressure. Every launch so far has been a practice session to insure the perfection of this stage. Once we release these balloons, the first victims should be reported in about twenty-four hours. Bubonic plague will sweep the eastern seaboard in a matter of hours. Then we make demands for ten million in gold and immunity from arrest, or the nation will be saturated. Of course, those demands will be a sham, merely a safeguard in the eventuality the authorities locate us too soon. But within three days, the nation's leaders should be on their knees, begging us to relent. From there on, *we own this country.*"

Chapter 16

BLACK DEATH

Ava hissed out silent death to one of the exterior guards. The man crumpled to the ground, brief tremors causing him to thrash quietly for several seconds. The Penetrator moved off to his left to locate his second target.

Thornesby had called in all his henchmen, those of the execution squad as well as other men connected in one way or another with the doctor's mad enterprise. From what he was able to observe, the Penetrator estimated that some fifteen men, not counting Wen and Thornesby, now occupied the farm. Learning from previous experience, they now had three perimeter guards out, watching all approaches. None of the men remained stationary but walked constantly in loose figure-eight patterns that provided overlapping fields of view at each extreme edge of their passage.

The Penetrator located the next roving patrol

and dispatched him neatly. He'd have to hurry to catch the last one before the others were noticed as missing and an alarm given. This pursuit, moving from the concealment of weed-grown fence lines to stacks of baled hay and on to outbuildings, resembled a silent, if deadly, game of hide-and-seek. Ava was a weapon ideally suited to this sort of action.

Created from a sketch of Mark's by Professor Haskins and an engineering-oriented machinist friend, the gas-powered, silent pistol fired one of two types of darts. The .22 caliber projectiles were modeled on the *Cap-chur Dart* system and injected a sleepytime potion of Pentothal and M-99 tranquilizer in a solution of di-methyl-sulfoxide, the super lubricant. The knockout darts also contained a mild neurotoxin that caused nearly instantaneous spasms that left victims help-less. Or a change in loads provided deadly cu-rarine, a derivative of the South American poison, also speeded into the blood by DMSO. True to its designers' intentions, Ava whispered the third guard to the ground, never to rise again. The Penetrator was ready to make his assault on the barn.

"Okay, men," Creighton Thornesby com-manded. "Let's take those six that are ready out-side so we can finish inflating them and begin the launch."

Two lab technicians grabbed a gently swaying balloon and walked it carefully to the end wall.

The odd-colored, elongated, five foot-diameter bag wobbled obscenely between them. As they opened the wide double doors, they stepped headlong into a close-range shotgun blast!

Shirt fronts and faces of both men were suddenly red spotted with a .28 caliber lead disease that mangled them to death. They fell away from the opening, their hands releasing the flaccid but slightly buoyant burden they carried. The balloon bobbed up and backward, out of sight and range inside the barn. Creighton Thornesby yelled something unintelligible in surprise and slammed shut one of the wide barn doors. Hal, always trustworthy, snatched up a pistol and ran to secure the other panel.

The Penetrator sent two more rounds through the opening before Hal had it closed. He had the temporary satisfaction of hearing muffled curses and tinkling cascades of breaking glass. Then he was taking return fire from the hayloft and ground-floor windows. Jumping to one side, in back of a high-wheeled hay wagon, the Penetrator took careful aim over the empty bed and blasted a pane of glass and the man behind it out of existence. Mark cycled the pump action and swiveled the barrel, looking for a new target.

Suddenly a man burst from a small side door, his hands out before him, empty. "Hey, man, don't shoot. Holy Christ, don't shoot! You know what's inside there?"

The Penetrator let the terrified man go, his

frightened running blending into the twilight dimness as four more deserters joined him. Then Mark sprinted to the opposite end of the wagon. He was lined up with the open door, which had banged back against the outside wall.

Jumping up, he blasted three loads of No. 4 buckshot from the hip toward the hayloft as covering fire while he dashed to the opening. Another three-inch Magnum 12-gauge round came from the shoulder, aimed randomly into the interior as the Penetrator entered the building. *Spanging* metal and spattering glass crescendoed into oblivion as the pellets struck the culture cabinet on the far wall. The Penetrator had little time to worry about that as a slug thudded into the wood above his head. He turned in that direction as a bullet bit deeply into his flesh.

Mark staggered backward as the jacketed soft point .32-20 Winchester slug tunneled a hot trail of agony through the inside top of his left armpit. The lead-tipped round had expanded to only double its size when it exited from his back, ripping out a fat thumb-sized chunk of meat triple the diameter of the entry wound. As he rolled, as if with a slow, heavy punch, Mark looked upward, eyes and shotgun muzzle tracking to where a man stood at the edge of the haymow.

One of the men who had been shooting at the Penetrator from the second-floor level had turned inward to counter his rush. The marksman had time for two hurried shots from his lever-action carbine before retribution caught up with him.

The Mossberg bellowed fiercely in the confined space of the barn. Twenty-seven pellets struck the man in his crotch and stomach, several more entering his chest. He was flung backward, to crumple lifelessly in a pile of aged, rotting hay. But just as the Penetrator had triggered off the gunman's *coup de grâce*, the unwieldly, flaccid skin of the partially inflated weather balloon wobbled into the edge of the shot pattern.

Four pellets punched through the rubbery hide, but it was enough to expel the contents with a rush. For an instant, stunned terror held in the barn. Then silence was broken by a whimper from Hal, who propelled himself from the cover of a horse stall, driven by his horrible knowledge of what the balloon contained. Firing wildly with a Browning Highpower 9mm automatic, Hal raced for the door.

The wound in the area of his shoulder had incapacitated the Penetrator's left arm. He was no longer able to accurately operate the Mossberg He laid it aside, drawing his .45 Star PD as Hal bore down on him, pistol blazing. Two slugs caught Hal dead center in the throat and face, stopping his frenzied charge and dropping him to the floor on suddenly slack legs. Two more shots echoed in the old barn, from opposite directions. Neither came close, but the Penetrator preferred to go hunting rather than play a sitting duck.

Blood trickled down Mark's side as he dodged between building supports and stalls, working his way to one end of the barn. A misstep set a clatter up from a discarded singletree, which was answered by another pair of bullets. He moved on, now watching the ground for obstacles as much as the open spaces of the interior for enemies. As he moved through the semi-darkness he had time to consider the light pinpoints of moisture that had tingled coolly on his skin after shooting the balloon. Whatever Creighton Thornesby planned to release on the public had infected him and everyone in the immediate area. He saw movement and fired instinctively.

A man let out a yelp of pain and slammed back against the wall, one hand holding his side. "Go on, kill me you bastard. Kill me!" he raged, bringing up his left hand, a pistol held unsteadily in it. He triggered off a single shot before the Penetrator granted his last wish.

A flat-nosed, 200-grain Hensley and Gibbs SWC lump of home-cast lead punched out the lab technician's left eye and exploded his brain into sloppy fragments before it removed a large chunk of skull from behind his right ear. Silence followed his crashing fall to the floor.

But the Penetrator had little time to enjoy the momentary cessation of hostilities. Muffled, furtive sounds came from the far end of the barn, and Mark turned to see three men fling open the wide double doors and run desperately away. He sent a slug zinging after them to speed them along, then turned back to his task of finding the man he knew must remain.

The Penetrator didn't find Creighton Thornes-

164

by, though. As he worked his way across the dangerous ground at the center of the barn, Thornesby was making good his break through the door in the opposite wall. Who the Penetrator located was Theophilous Wen.

Early in the battle Wen had taken three shotgun pellets high in the chest. He had leaked a considerable amount of blood, internally as well as externally. Wen was weak and barely able to hold onto the M-11 .22 long rifle-caliber submachine gun he waveringly brought up before him. He got off a ragged burst though before the Penetrator's reflexes planted two .45 bullets into nearly the same hole in Wen's forehead. The fanatic One-Worlder from SIE would plot to enslave the people no more. Mark was changing magazines in the Star PD when he heard the sound of a starter motor grinding outside the barn.

Mark dashed through the open door, eyes adjusting to the outer darkness. Fifty feet from the barn Mark saw a car, a tensed pigeon-breasted form crouched over the steering wheel. In his anxiety to escape, Creighton Thornesby had flooded the engine. His frantic efforts to start the car turned to panic as the Penetrator advanced on him with a measured tread.

Creighton Thornesby had watched the Penetrator's shotgun blast destroy the culture cabinet with only a slight tremor of worry. Their only supply of antitoxin for the deadly plague bacillus was in that locked container. Yet, as far as he could see, there simply could be no way for anyone to become contaminated. Then the Penetrator had ruptured the balloon while exchanging fire with the man who wounded him.

In that instant, Creighton Thornesby knew terror as no man had comprehended it before. The entire inside of the barn—and everyone in it—had been exposed to the plague. It was a horrid, strangling death that robbed a man of his last measure of dignity. It was reputed to cause pain so excruciating that the most exotic Oriental torture paled to insignificance beside it.

Developed by the army for germ warfare, it was synthesized from known strains of the Black Plague, intensified, and given a far shorter incubation period. The ABC researchers had also come up with a way to make it transmittable by airborne means, so that no longer did they have to reply upon a plentiful supply of rats, each with a mass of fleas that played host to the ghastly bacillus. Out at Dougway they had also produced an antitoxin to be given friendly troops and populations.

Thornesby had produced cultures of the special strain in the same means used by the army. He had also extracted a small quantity of the antidote—just enough for his own men, trusting to the army to rush large shipments of the serum to the East Coast to contain the plague. Now the life-saving fluid was gone, blown into spatters on a wall by this unbelievable nemesis who had so unerringly tracked his operation to the ground. He had to get somewhere, turn himself in for treatment before it was too late.

"The game's over, Thornesby. Give it up," the Penetrator said softly as he neared Thornesby's auto.

Resigned to the fact the car would not start, Creighton Thornesby's mind gave way to his own terror. "Finish it, damn you. Shoot me and kill yourself. *Don't you know what you've done?* That balloon was loaded with *Pasteurella pestis.* That's right! Bubonic plague—the Black Death, for God's sake! You've infected us all, and we're not going to live another thirty-six hours. Believe me, they will be the most hideous minutes of our lives, unless—unless you kill us now."

"There has to be a cure," the Penetrator said, taking a step closer.

"No. None of the usual things work. This is a special strain. I had some antitoxin, but you destroyed that too. Only—only the army has a way to arrest the plague. Now that none of the balloons were launched, they won't release it. Top secret stuff, you know. Wait and see if you want, but not me. I'll make you kill me if I have to."

Thornesby jerkily raised the muzzle of a .38 Colt snub nose and pulled clumsily on the trigger. His hand was shaking so badly, though, that one bullet plowed into the dirt a yard from the Penetrator's feet while the other went singing off toward the moon. The Penetrator returned fire, one slug smashing through the metal panel into Thornesby's knee, the other imbedding itself in the thick metal of the door post.

Mark reached the car and opened the door violently. He slapped the gun from Thornesby's hand and dragged him out. Mark looked with disgust at the man he held. Lips curling, he spoke harshly.

"No. I don't think I will kill you. I'm going to tie you up and leave you here. Let's see if the army can find you in time." He turned from the helpless man to find a length of cord.

"Please! I can't stand to die this way!" Thornesby begged.

The Penetrator paused, thinking. If the army did get antitoxin to Thornesby in time and treated him, it was obvious he would never stand trial. He was as nutty as they came. Six months in a mental hospital and, given the sob-sister, weak-minded courts of today, Thornesby could be back on the streets to menace innocent people again. It was much like the question of the president's analyst. The security of the nation could not be trusted in the hands of some flitty shrink. He turned back to Thornesby.

"I've changed my mind," the Penetrator said as he raised the Star PD. He should be moved by mercy, but he felt certain of his own death;

Thornesby's terror was too genuine to discount. Yet he couldn't leave the books unbalanced.

One slug, neatly placed between Creighton Thornesby's eyes, did it.

EPILOGUE

And thus the whirligig of time brings in his revenges.
— Shakespeare

Strange and tragic as it may seem in this modern age of miracle drugs, clinics, and treatment centers, there is no place for a man who has a fatal and communicable disease to go. There is no haven, that is, if the man so afflicted is considered a fugitive by the same authorities who hold the sole cure to his illness. The Penetrator accepted this anomaly of our progressive world stoically, if not philosophically. Then he set about helping himself.

First there came the matter of loose ends. He set the plague-ridden barn afire with white phosphorous grenades. From the car that Creighton Thornesby had attempted to use to escape, he removed an attaché case stuffed with $475,000 in large bills. The money would help offset operating expenses. At a roadside service station, he called the sheriff's office from a phone booth, informing the dispatcher that four men with a highly contagious disease were on the loose in the county. Then questioned further, Mark told the officer that they were carriers of bubonic plague.

"They're on foot," he concluded. "You won't have any trouble finding the center of the search area. There's a barn there blazing like mad. The people responsible for your livestock sickness were cooking up their germs there." His last words insured a prompt response.

Mark drove to Mohawk airport in Rhinelander, locked the rental car, and placed a hand-lettered notice on it. "Warning!" it read. "Bubonic plague! This car must be checked and cleared by U.S. Public Health Service before being touched by anyone." He climbed wearily into the Mooney and headed westward.

From the airplane the Penetrator telephoned the Stronghold. He filled the professor in and asked to talk to Red Eagle. He told the old Cheyenne medicine man of his physical condition and asked for help. Red Eagle named a place in the sacred Black Hills of South Dakota. Mark agreed to meet him there and ended the conversation. He checked his charts, selected the course he wanted to take, and turned the flying job over to the auto-pilot. He felt weary to death in every part of his body.

The Penetrator lingered fifteen days, fighting the effects of bubonic plague with the help of Red Eagle. Few persons had ever before endured the ravages of the deadly killer of the Middle Ages for so long. Delirium, fever, and suppurating sores grew and retreated only to come on again as the sacred powers of *Sho-tu-ça* and the healing potions of the medicine man's art warred with the ominous bacillus.

The crisis came on the nineteenth day. Visons of thousands of SIE members, marching in close ranks through the streets of American cities, their red banners waving above them, filled Mark's head. His body, packed in the last of winter's snows, throbbed with fever, and his vital forces sank to their lowest. How many more, like Theophilus Wen, had managed to escape? The thought haunted his agony.

No longer able to aid in the fight to save his own life, the burden of healing fell entirely on Red Eagle. With prayers and ritual, the old Indian called forth the deadly forces at work in Mark's body, took them to himself, and then— cast them away. In that instant it seemed as if the fever abated a degree or two, the purplish-black color of the disfiguring buboes on Mark's face, throat, and body lightened imperceptibly, and the grotesque swelling began to subside. It was a start.

Now new prayers were needed. Red Eagle, aided by the most powerful medicine singer of the Pine Ridge Sioux, worked without rest, day and night, fasting and working the secret arts that gave back men's lives. There was no room for negative images in the minds of the healers, yet it seemed as if there remained little chance.

On the twenty-second day, Mark Hardin opened clear eyes to find that he lay on a pine bough bed in a damp cave. A buffalo skull, well preserved and ancient, rested on the stone floor at his feet, its crumbling horns decorated with feathers and bits of fur, strips of colored ribbon. His head no longer swirled with frightening visions and scenes of his own death. He was weak, but well. Mark struggled to raise himself on one elbow, sighed, and fell back.

"Yes, you survived." Red Eagle's voice changed, became stern, like a parent chiding an errant child, *"But don't ever do that again."* He rose from a woven reed backrest, where he had been sitting cross-legged. He crossed to a stone jug and returned with a cloth that dripped cool water. Kneeling, he bathed Mark's face, then smiled.

"Next time there may not be anyone alive who knows how to heal you."

Mark's voice came out a breathy croak, the weak cry of a starving kitten. "I—I promise I'll never get infected with bubonic plague again."

Two days later, Mark got up and around, yet he felt reluctant to leave the haven of this medicine cave. Not a single item of modern origin was at hand. Everything had to be done in a sacred manner to effect the cure, so nothing could be present that wasn't done in the ancient and sacred way. It was restful, peaceful, with a calming sense of continuity with the past and future. Mark reveled in it like an epicure at a

Tiberian orgy. The cave, Mark had learned, was located on Harney Mountain, a spot sacred to the Sioux since Colonel Harney had turned cannon fire on Little Thunder's women and children. It had become a place for quiet contemplation, a Spirit Place, holy and revered. An ideal locale for healing—a place where the Penetrator would have liked to stay forever. Yet consciousness of the present and the real world outside could not escape him indefinitely.

On the evening of the twenty-fifty day, Mark sat outside the cave, watching the last crimson rays of the setting sun turn sentinel pines into black paper cutout silhouettes. There was still a coolness in the air that made his wounded shoulder ache. Sighing heavily, Mark thought of the pair of season tickets to the Green Bay Packers' home games that had been arranged for him by Olie Swensen. He doubted that he'd ever be able to use them.

Thoughts of Olie made Mark think also of John Foxkiller and Joey Runningraven—and of Karl Kruger, the dairy farmer whose murder had signaled the start of the downfall of Creighton Thornesby's mad design. What a waste of life. They had been the real losers, four men dying without knowing the contribution they had made to saving the lives of millions. They were at rest now, buried with all the other innocents who had died because of someone's greed and ambition. Perhaps, Mark thought, he too could rest while recovering his strength and prowess.

But that turned out to be a forlorn hope. Late the next afternoon Red Eagle returned from the post office at Pine Ridge with a bulky package. Reluctantly Mark opened it and began to digest the data Professor Haskins had sent to him. It was a grim picture. The latest twist in the Mexican Brown situation indicated that the importation of heroin from this as-yet-unknown source had reached monumental proportions.

The Penetrator read and reread the material, knowing that something would have to be done about it soon—and in a manner only he could handle.

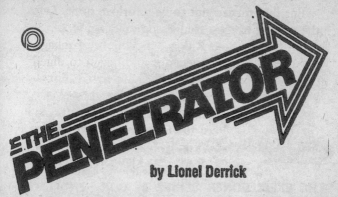

THE PENETRATOR

by Lionel Derrick

Mark Hardin. Discharged from the army, after service in Vietnam. His military career was over. But *his* war was just beginning. His reason for living and reason for dying became the same—to stamp out crime and corruption wherever he finds it. He is deadly; he is unpredictable; and he is dedicated. He is The Penetrator!

Read all of him in:

THE INCREDIBLE ACTION PACKED SERIES

DEATH MERCHANT

by Joseph Rosenberger

His name is Richard Camellion, he's a master of disguise, deception and destruction. He does what the CIA and FBI cannot do.

Order	Title	Book #	Price
# 1	THE DEATH MERCHANT	P211	$ .95
# 2	OPERATION OVERKILL	P245	$ .95
# 3	THE PSYCHOTRON PLOT	P117	$ .95
# 4	CHINESE CONSPIRACY	P168	$ .95
# 5	SATAN STRIKE	P182	$ .95
# 6	ALBANIAN CONNECTION	P670	$1.25
# 7	CASTRO FILE	P264	$ .95
# 8	BILLIONAIRE MISSION	P339	$ .95
# 9	THE LASER WAR	P399	$ .95
#10	THE MAINLINE PLOT	P473	$1.25
#11	MANHATTAN WIPEOUT	P561	$1.25
#12	THE KGB FRAME	P642	$1.25
#13	THE MATO GROSSO HORROR	P705	$1.25
#14	VENGEANCE OF THE GOLDEN HAWK	P796	$1.25
#15	THE IRON SWASTIKA PLOT	P823	$1.25
#16	INVASION OF THE CLONES	P857	$1.25
#17	THE ZEMLYA EXPEDITION	P880	$1.25